FORCE OF NATURE

A CARPINO NOVEL

BRYNNE ASHER

FORCE OF NATURE

A Carpino Novel
Brynne Asher

Published by Brynne Asher
BrynneAsherBooks@gmail.com

Keep up with me on Facebook for news and upcoming
books
https://www.facebook.com/BrynneAsherAuthor

Join my reader group to keep up with my latest news
Brynne Asher's Beauties

Keep up with all Brynne Asher books and news
Sign up for my newsletter here

Edited by Hadley Finn
Cover Design by Dark Waters Covers

OTHER BOOKS BY BRYNNE ASHER

The Carpino Series

Overflow – The Carpino Series, Book 1

Beautiful Life – The Carpino Series, Book 2

Athica Lane – The Carpino Series, Book 3

Until Avery – A Carpino Series Crossover Novella

Killers Series

Vines – A Killers Novel, Book 1

Paths – A Killers Novel, Book 2

Gifts – A Killers Novel, Book 3

Veils – A Killers Novel, Book 4

Scars – A Killers Novel, Book 5

Souls – A Killers Novel, Book 6

Until the Tequila – A Killers Crossover Novella

The Killers, The Next Generation

Levi, Asa's son

The Dillon Sisters

Deathly by Brynne Asher

Damaged by Layla Frost

The Montgomery Series

Bad Situation – The Montgomery Series, Book 1

Broken Halo – The Montgomery Series, Book 2

Standalones

Blackburn

CONTENTS

1. The Asshole   1
2. Notifications   11
3. Say Less   21
4. Logan with a Lowercase p   31
5. Perfect Storm   41
6. Delete   51
7. Scratch the Itch   61
8. Catastrophic   77
9. Irrational and Unjustified and Completely Senseless   83
10. Fuck the Numbers   91
11. Vulnerable   97
12. My Fire Needs Wood   105
13. Cheers to Gray Sweatpants   113
14. The Forestry Commission   119
15. Score One for Math Nerds   131
16. Chicken   139
17. Go With Your Gut   145
18. Open Ended   157
19. Airport   163
20. Code Red   169
21. Mine   177
22. Happy Scale   187
23. A Carpino Christmas   197
Epilogue   205

About the Author   209
What to Read Next   211

*To my OG readers, who embraced my Carpinos in the beginning.
This is for you.*

Let's take it back to where it all started…

ONE
THE ASSHOLE

Demi

"Do it."

"No. I'm not doing it."

"Forget that nightmare ever happened and jump back in the saddle, Demi. You know, carpe diem—seize the day. It's what everyone says on Instagram."

"Like I care about Instagram, and I know you don't either. I danced too close to the fire and got burned. I don't trust my own instincts anymore. I think I need to sit out the next decade."

"Just one more swipe. For shits and giggles."

"Nope. Never again."

"Give it to me. I'll pick for you."

My eyes widen to the size of the china saucers my grandma serves with tea when Posey reaches for my phone. "Like hell—"

But before I have a chance to delete the app or stuff my cell down my bra—like that would stop Posey—she plucks my cell from my sweaty palms and backs away from me in her ugly Christmas sweater. Artie, the owner of Peak 7 Local, a bar on the main drag, always hosts the annual Christmas party. He opens the back room for the town residents only. It's usually one of my favorite times of the year. But given my current fiasco, I'm done. I want to go home and hibernate until the holiday rush is over when I can hit the slopes without getting mowed over by wannabe shredders who really have no clue what they're doing.

"Give me that." I lunge around the high-top table we've been drinking at for the last hour.

She's faster than me, and her thumb scrolls at the speed of light as her eyes light up in mischief. "Ooooh. Here's a good one."

"Don't—"

But I can't stop her. The moment she swipes, my stomach drops. Posey's green eyes land on me and they scream *winner, winner, chicken dinner*. Damn her. "There. Tall, dark, and, from his profile pic, broody as hell—which matches your current state of mind perfectly. Also, I widened your location. That guy lives far, far away from Winter Falls. No need to worry about another stalker. And since we just reported the last guy who can't take a hint from Daddy Sheriff, all will be good in the hood."

Ugh.

She tosses my cell, but she's still as clumsy as she was on our sixth-grade softball team. I grab it at the last second, and it gets tangled in the mini strand of lights on my ugly grandpa sweater. But she doesn't care and turns to pick up her White Elephant present.

"This will be a fun experiment. A long-distance relationship might be just what the matchmaker ordered. And I know you, Demi. You're too nice to delete the app since I swiped right."

"You're wrong. I'm deleting it now." Who am I kidding? She's right, I'll never delete it now. But I refuse to admit it, and pretend to scroll through my phone as I pull up the profile Posey just exposed me to like a bad rash.

I cringe.

Not because he isn't hot.

He is.

Like, scorching.

And she wasn't kidding about the tall and dark part. He claims to be six-three and has a lush head of wavy, dark hair that makes me green with envy. I doubt he needs five bottles of products and enough hairspray to put a hole in the ozone layer to get those waves to behave, like I do.

His profile picture is different from any other I've seen. His crisp blue dress shirt is loose at the neck, rolled at the sleeves, and has a day's worth of wrinkles. It's somewhat of an action shot as he stalks down a city street. But what's most shocking is the frown marring his perfect olive-skin and five-o'clock-shadowed face.

And the middle finger he's using to flip off the camera. Though, the veins running up his thick forearm and disappearing into his rolled sleeve don't suck.

Still, he chose this picture to market himself to single women.

What the hell?

This guy is from New York City—specifically, Manhattan. That might explain his foul mood. I'm somewhat relieved. The Big Apple isn't exactly half a world away, but it's far enough I don't have to worry about him turning into a Sambal VanDervleté, the reason for my current life crisis. I should've known better than swiping on his profile. VanDervleté sounds like a villain from a children's novel, not a mechanical engineer from the next town over.

No, the angry guy from Manhattan is Logan Carpino.

Wait. This could be worse than a fictional villain.

Carpino screams mafia—and not the soft, PG-network-TV kind of mafia. This guy could be the real, legit hard-core premium-cable-channel mafia.

And if his picture isn't scary enough—while hot—his profile couldn't be more confusing.

And, quite frankly, alarming.

Gender: Pure fucking male, with all the extras, if you know what I mean.

Relationship Status: Unapologetically single and never been close to marriage.

Age: Mid-thirties and thriving.

Ethnicity: Italian-American Perfection. Yes, with a capital P.

Born: Omaha, Nebraska. Don't knock it. We have the College World Series.

Current Residence: Higher in the sky than you can afford.

Income: You can't even fathom.

Highest Level of Education: It doesn't matter. I'm smarter than ninety-nine percent of the population. The other one percent can kiss my ass. Still—it must be mentioned—my MBA is from Wharton.

Children: Billions of genetically perfect humans, just waiting to be set free.

Interests: Golf—playing and watching, kicking ass at pickup basketball, math, Fortune Magazine, and my Perfect hair. Note the P.

Hobbies: Irritating my administrative assistant and siblings.

Occupation: Businessy stuff.

Is this guy for real?

Businessy stuff?

Pretentious much? And aren't we all in some sort of business? I mean, I'm in the business of hacking, but my profile says computer programmer. I don't need to attract the kind of people who would be interested in me solely for my skills. Having a mechanical engineer as a stalker is bad enough.

But, seriously, what an arrogant ass! Who puts themselves out there like that? Most assholes are assholes enough to at least fake being an asshole. No one advertises their asshole-ness like this.

It has to be a fake account.

Yes. That has to be it. The knot in my chest untangles and the thought of a repeat of Sam VanDervleté happening all over again disintegrates into thin air.

I exhale. I think I'm good.

"I'm out of here. I have a project that's due before Christmas. It's late and my voice will be toast tomorrow unless I get some rest." Posey's voice is the most beautiful I've ever heard. It's melodic, smooth, and, yes, even sexy. She has a way of making you want to sit and listen to her for hours. Which I do all the time. She utilizes her gifts and makes a killing narrating audiobooks.

"I'm not speaking to you for at least a week," I mutter and toss my phone in my bag. That's a lie. I could never go that long without Posey. "It's not like you're the queen of putting yourself out there. You suck as much as I do … and don't try and pretend you don't. You're never allowed to touch my phone again."

She has the nerve to laugh. "It'll be fun to see what happens with that one."

I focus my glare on her. "It's a fake account, and you know it."

Her expression turns smug. "So you didn't delete the app and you were curious enough to look. He's hot. And he's not hiding the fact he's a dick. He's put it out there for the world to see. You've gotta give him credit—that's worth the swipe on its own."

"I'm not giving him anything."

She shrugs her coat up her arms and wraps it around herself. "You might be happier if you give it away more often."

I shake my head. "I hate you. Goodbye. Drive safe. I'll see you next year, since I'm unfriending you for the rest of this one."

She saunters out as she yells over her shoulder, "Whatever. You know you'll call me tomorrow. And just for fun, let your magic fingertips do their thing and research the Italian hottie with a capital P. I want to know if he's real or not. As much as you want to pretend otherwise, you do too."

I wave her off before the heavy, paneled door shuts, and she disappears into the cold, dark night.

It's colder than normal, and a front is forecasted to hit the mountains. The *Farmer's Almanac* promised this winter would be a bad one. So far, they missed the mark and the ski slopes don't have nearly as much powder as they usually do.

"You need a ride, Demi?" Artie calls from behind the bar.

I shake my head and smile. "I'm good. Dad is on duty tonight and said he'd give me a ride since it's so late."

He nods, and his jaw goes hard. "Heard about your stalker. You've gotta take that shit seriously."

"It wasn't that bad. He just…" I do my best to play it off because, no matter how bad it was, I don't like the attention. "He wasn't ready to call it quits. Stalker is a strong definition. I'm fine now."

In other words, I'm fine now that the county sheriff paid Sam a visit. My dad promised me that Sam is not fine, though. He was shaken up when Dad threatened him with an order of protection.

"That's not what I heard," Artie sing-songs as he washes glasses. "I heard your daddy threatened him within an inch of his life to stay far away from his little girl."

Well, so much for playing down the drama, and I'm hardly little. I'm twenty-eight. "It's over. That's all that matters."

"Heard you met him on some new-fangled dating app. Stay away from those, Demi. Nothing but freaks out there. You need to settle down with someone here in Winter Falls, where you belong."

I've known Artie my entire life, so I don't roll my eyes. I love him. He coached my soccer team for years and is a family friend. But if someone else tells me what to do tonight…

"There's my girl."

Cold air swirls through the bar. When I turn, Sheriff Joel Benjamin stands tall and wide in the open door, snowflakes glinting in the street lights behind him. "Hey, Dad."

"Joel!" Artie yells.

Dad lifts his chin and turns his attention back to me. "You ready? We got a call on the other side of the mountain. Someone got a flat. I'll drop you home on the way."

"Yeah. I'm tired and have a long day tomorrow." I tug my purse up my shoulder and turn to the bar. "Bye, Artie, and thanks! Fun night."

I head to the door and my dad circles his arm around my shoulders. "Fun, huh? Am I going to have to threaten anyone else?"

I think about my cell phone burning a hole in my purse. I was itching to research the Italian hottie before Posey suggested it. I still don't think there's any way the asshole can be real. At least not anyone who wants to be taken seriously. A woman would be mad to take that on.

Logan Carpino, the fictional asshole-slash-mafia boss can bother some other unassuming woman.

I'm done with online dating.

TWO
NOTIFICATIONS

Logan

I control myself, even though I want to frown.

My phone vibrates on the table in front of me as I'm addressing the board of directors.

Cells are to be used when one needs them, but should never interrupt my thoughts, my work … or, most importantly, my life.

My notifications are turned off. For everything. Phone calls, texts, and emails. When you're a Carpino, it's damn near impossible to get anything done when your notifications are buzzing your ass every five minutes. My family is that much of a pain at times. They're relentless.

Unlike the rest of the world, I use my cell to keep track of time. Time is money. I'm obsessed with the latter, so the prior is equally important to me. Wasting time is wasting money.

Other than my banking and investment portfolios,

the only apps I use are for weather, sports, and workouts.

I go to those when I have time at the end of the day or if I'm stuck in traffic. Otherwise, my assistant manages my messages and emails. She knows my priorities and feeds me what I need, when I need it.

But even from her, I do not have my fucking notifications on because she's always on the same continent as me. Hell, she's usually in the next room. So my phone vibrating on the conference table is a first.

I flip to the last slide of my presentation and look to my audience—a group of men and women who hated me before I even stepped foot in their country two weeks ago. But then again, they usually do when I first come onto a project. They'll come around eventually.

Or, they won't and they'll hate me forever. I don't give a shit. Either way, their company was about to go under, and we're the reason they still have jobs. It's not my fault their prior owners and board had their heads up their asses and fucked up what should've been a profitable corporation.

Mergers and acquisitions.

It's what I know, and quite frankly, I'm a killer in my field. It's why I rose to the top of my firm. I've made my company more money in the last decade than they made in the last thirty years. We buy corporations that are about to go under, fix them—which usually means cutting the fat at the top—and make them a lean, mean, cash-generating machine.

Then we sell them.

It's the American way.

Even if I am Down Under.

I wrap the meeting and the team of what used to

comprise a good chunk of middle management files out. Like usual, the first thing we did when I landed in Australia was cut the bulky overhead. The men and women who just sat through my directives are the ones who will run this ship and help make it profitable. They're still here, which makes them the best. They'll make a great team when we're all said and done. They might be shell-shocked right now, but in a couple of months, they'll be running this multimillion-dollar corporation and have it on its way to its first billion. And that's when we'll sell.

They're the bones that got it to where it is today— it was top management who fucked things up.

Usually is.

Instead of looking out at Sydney Harbour and the Opera House as I've gotten used to over the last few weeks, I reach for my phone that has kept me and our management meeting on schedule.

Because time is money, I'm certainly not going to profit from a time-sucking dating app.

Like the notification that just popped on my screen.

Congratulations! Someone thinks you're a Force of Nature.

What the fuck?

I mean, of course I'm a force of nature.

I don't need my damn phone to tell me this.

But what the hell?

"You've got twenty minutes before your conference call with IT and you can't be late. I squeezed them in today. With the time difference, I won't be surprised if they'll be in their pajamas for the video conference."

I slide my phone into my pocket and ignore the digital intrusion on my time. "What are they warning me about this week?"

Lina has been with the company for over twenty years and with me for the last three. Her kids are in college, and she likes to travel. Her husband can work from anywhere, so he tags along. They both get to work and see the world, and I get the best of the best. So much so, Lina and her husband have front and center seats at the Sydney Opera House tonight courtesy of yours truly.

I need Lina happy so she'll continue to put up with me and keep me organized.

See? I am a force of nature. I don't need a cell phone to tell me so.

"Extending the cybersecurity to the offices here. Since you're the lead in Australia, they insisted on the live chat. I just emailed you the files." Lina pokes at her tablet as she speaks then stands. "I'm going to grab a sandwich. Can I bring you anything? The afternoon is packed, and this is your only chance to eat."

I grab my laptop and move to the office I've made mine. "You know what I hate. Anything else is good. I appreciate it."

I close myself in the space with floor-to-ceiling windows that look out over the Harbour and iconic Opera House. I'm about to open the files from Lina, but the lone notification sitting on my phone waiting to be clicked gets under my skin.

Instead of preparing for my next meeting, I open a new browser tab and type in *Someone thinks you're a Force of Nature*.

Well, fuck me.

The top five search results all point to the same place.

A dating app—*Force of Nature*.

How the hell…

Oh, shit. No they didn't.

I grab my cell and press go on my damn brother.

It goes to voicemail.

I dial again.

Voicemail.

I text him – ***Answer your fucking phone, asswipe.***

I call again.

He finally answers. "Jackass. Did you forget it's the middle of the night here?"

"I don't give a shit, Sleeping Beauty. What the hell did you do, Grant?"

Grant is four years older. Avery is the baby of the family and five years younger than me. Grant is normal—went to college, got married, had kids, made our parents peachy-fucking-keen happy. Avery, on the other hand, dropped out of college, was literally knocked up and married before she could legally drink. But she also has two GRAMMY awards sitting on the mantle over the fireplace of her Nashville McMansion. She and her husband, Link, have had two kids while she writes award-winning songs that A-List singers are gagging over.

Me?

I'm the middle one, and although I've grown out of my awkward middle-kid syndrome, I still manage to be the favorite purely because of my overachiever syndrome. Though, my mom is still on my ass about settling down and having a shit ton of germ bombs she so affectionately calls grandkids.

I hear the smugness coming through the phone even though I can tell I woke him. "I have no idea what you're talking about."

I stalk back and forth in front of the windows. "My

15

phone. What the hell did you do when you were here last week?"

Lina's husband isn't the only one who takes advantage of our travel. My family has been crashing my business trips for years. The company always puts me up in pretty sweet accommodations since I'm on site for months at a time, and the Carpinos don't even ask. They do what they always do and descend upon you like a wake of vultures.

Grant and his wife, Clara, and Avery and her husband, Link, visited for a week. The only reason my parents didn't join the party is because they were tasked with babysitting the germ bombs—also known as my nieces and nephews.

"I don't know what you're talking about."

"You put a dating app on my fucking phone, fuckwad."

It starts out low, but his guttural laugh rumbles through the line from the opposite hemisphere. "Did some poor woman actually swipe on you?"

I stop in the middle of the windows and drag a hand down my face. "I hate you."

He keeps laughing. "Hey, I didn't actually download the app, but I might've had something to do with setting up your profile. It was Link's idea. Wake him up and cuss him out."

I shake my head and stare out at the boats. "Dammit."

"What does she look like?"

"I have no clue. I haven't opened it."

"Send me a screenshot. I want to know what woman in her right mind would pick you. Or, the you we created. Which is really the real you. So real, I don't know what anyone would see in you, unless the woman is a masochist."

My head pops up, and I demand, "What did you say about me?"

"Nothing that isn't the truth." He has the nerve to yawn in my ear while describing how he and my brother-in-law invaded my privacy. "We only put the truth. All the truth, and nothing but the——"

"I'm going to punch you in the balls the next time I see you," I interrupt.

"What does she look like?"

"Are you even paying attention? I don't know. I'm too busy being pissed because I've been betrayed by my own fucking family."

"It was a great idea, and the drinks had nothing to do with it. It's not my fault you put your phone down when it wasn't locked to go work the night away instead of watching rugby with us. Looking back, you're responsible for this. We were just drunk on vacation."

"On vacation," I echo. I cannot fucking believe him.

"Lighten up. You could use a vacation of your own. Hell, leave now and find the woman who swiped your profile. Anyone who would choose you in a sea of bachelors needs an award. Or therapy."

"Now I'm going to have to message whoever this woman is and explain what happened. I'm going to look like an ass."

"Oh, trust me. Once you see your profile, you'll know that's already the case."

"Fuck," I hiss.

There's a knock at my door. I motion for Lina to

come in but keep talking to Grant. "You're an asshole, and I hope I never see you again."

Lina bites back a smile as she sets a paper bag of food on the conference table in the corner of my office.

Grant isn't done. "Chill, little brotha. You never know, you might be thanking me when you make it back home and the perfect woman for some unknown reason thinks you're not the self-centered dumbass you've become. Do yourself a favor and entertain the idea. You never know, maybe the perfect storm will strike down *the* Logan Carpino. It'll be epic—the death of a bachelor."

I've had enough. "Do me a favor and relay my *fuck you* message to Link too."

"Come on, it was a joke—"

I don't wait for him to say more. I slam my cell to the conference table.

Lina smirks. "What did the Carpinos do now?"

"You don't want to know," I mutter. "But if I ever see my family again, I'm giving you my cell phone to lock away for safekeeping. They cannot be trusted."

"I can't wait to hear." She smiles big as she leans back, and I sign onto the video conference that I'm not looking forward to.

THREE
SAY LESS

Demi

"Gotcha," I whisper.

To no one.

Since I'm alone.

I might be alone but I'm not a loner. I like people. I like to be around people and socialize and go out and be a part of a community.

So don't ask me how I got here.

Alone, working from home in my dilapidated house that I can't afford to fix up yet because I spent all my money on the house and property itself. Location, location, location—it's the name of the game, especially in the mountains.

My house might suck, but my view does not. And that's what I paid for. Now I just need to fix up the house so it will be as pretty as the surrounding mountain ranges that go on forever.

There are days I wonder how I got here. Not to

Winter Falls. I was born here, went to college close by so I could live at home, and stayed here.

I mean here—on top of my mountain, sitting on my own land, *alone*.

I'm an independent contractor and work virtually. Outside of a random online-date-turned-into-stalker or a girls' night out, my life is my work and my mountain, yet it must be mentioned again, *alone*.

Which is why I work all the hours. I might as well. The more money I stuff away, the sooner I can gut my house.

And that brings me back to how I got here.

Video games.

If my big brothers weren't tearing up the slopes or kicking someone's ass in football, they were in front of a gaming console. I did what they did, besides the kicking-someone's-ass-in-football part.

I watched them. And then I bugged them enough to let me play. I not only got good, I got really good. I beat them, then I beat their friends, and then I beat strangers online. I studied the programs, learned their patterns, figured out how they were structured to challenge the best gamers.

I was accused of hacking into online games before I graduated high school.

Those accusations weren't without merit.

My degree in information technology was no surprise to anyone.

But my minor is in criminal justice.

Which is how I got here. Setting up technical infrastructures for corporations is boring. Providing support for those infrastructures is downright coma-inducing. And maintaining the safety of them? Well, that's sort of like being a mall cop.

But breaking into them?

And being paid to do it?

It's like I'm living the dream.

I have a passion and found a way to make money doing it. My only problem is that my passion is …

Lonely.

Still. I love to crawl into a corporate structure and virtually scream, "Boo, baby. I got you!"

It's more fun than any video game, ever.

My phone rings. I'm surprised it took as long as it did.

"This is Demi."

"Well, damn. I'll be the first to apologize. You actually did it."

I sit back in my chair and smile, but gloating is rude, especially to paying clients. "No need to apologize. I got hung up yesterday for a full seven hours. Kudos to you and your team. That doesn't happen often."

"Told my managers this was a waste of money, that we were solid. I was wrong and can admit it. I'm sorry."

He was an ass when the final contract was signed. He refused to give me any help, which I didn't ask for. When a company hires me to hack into their systems to find their weaknesses, I don't need help. They're paying me to do it like a real hacker would. But dealing with managers like him is pretty normal. "It's really okay."

"You sure you don't want a job? I'll make a position for you today," he goes on.

I've been offered more jobs than I can count at this point. "I've got a job, but thanks. In my line of work, that's the highest form of flattery."

"I still can't believe it. All it took was the first warning light and my team is in panic mode. When will I get your full report?"

"I'll have it to you in a couple of days. Now that I'm in, I need to look for other areas of weakness. I'll draw up my recommendations and be available for the next month as a consultant. It's part of my fee. You'll be squared away in no time."

"Thanks. I've got to settle my troops. They're blaming each other." His frustration turns into a resigned sigh. "Again, I'm sorry I thought your services were a waste of money. I might write you into my annual budget. You're definitely worth every penny. If someone really got into our systems and shut us down, we'd be at the top of every news site in the country."

Since they are the infrastructure that provides power to most of the northwest, he's not kidding.

"Don't go too hard on your team. It wasn't that easy. I'll be in touch."

"I look forward to the report, but I don't look forward to dealing with my boss."

We say our last goodbyes, and I'm about to set my phone down when I get another notification.

You have a message from your Force of Nature!

Oh, shit.

I figured since his profile couldn't be legit, ignoring it would make the whole thing go away.

I'm never hesitant with technology, but as if I'm tickling a ravenous shark, I reach out and lightly tap the message that most women would probably be excited to get.

I felt the same when Sam VanDervleté answered

my swipe, and that bought me a creepy stalker and weeks of drama.

The app opens, and I'm suddenly looking at what I assumed was a fake account. Or, at the very least, a joke.

The photo of the man who claims to be Logan Carpino glares back at me as he flips me off, with a message below his profile picture.

Logan Carpino – Not for nothing, but this was a mistake. No hard feelings.

Wow. No hard feelings?

Who does this guy think he is? If it's even a real guy behind the picture.

Bubbles appear, like he's getting ready to prove how many more ways he's an asshole before I even have the chance to respond.

I push my phone away and move back to my computer. Opening a new tab, I type in his name.

I not only get a hit, but I get pages of them, and I didn't even have to dig.

The first hit confirms his profile on the app. Logan Carpino, Senior Vice President, Mergers and Acquisitions Division for Andopolis Global, headquartered in New York City.

Other hits support the first. Articles in *Forbes*, *The New York Times*, *The Wall Street Journal*, and so many other business publications they would put a normal human to sleep. That's how boring they sound.

What isn't boring is an article from *The New Yorker* about the top twenty most eligible bachelors in Manhattan.

Hmm.

I'll come back to that one.

Instead, I go to the top of the search and click on images.

I am human after all.

More specifically, female.

And, after the most eligible bachelor article, hella curious.

A warmth ripples over my skin and makes the hairs on my arms stand at attention.

Because the Italian-American man who claims to be a capital P in most everything, has so many images, I can't decide which to select first.

Him – at a Yankees game sitting in a suite eating popcorn.

Him – posing with a petite woman, who's as pregnant as they come, while she holds a GRAMMY, of all things.

Him – standing on the Great Wall with another guy who resembles him. The other guy's hair might be close to perfect, but not with a capital P.

Him – wearing a three-piece suit that fits like a glove in front of the New York Stock Exchange.

Him – at New York Fashion Week sitting next to a redhead, looking so bored, he might be in physical pain.

And him – in the rumpled shirt, angry, flipping off the camera. The same picture he chose for his profile that shows off his beautifully veined forearm.

The pictures go on and on and on.

I sit back in my chair.

He's not fake? This can't be. But no one would steal a picture from the internet only to use that person's name.

I pick up my phone and let my fingers fly.

Me – Mistake? Like, your index finger slipped and you accidentally posted your profile on a dating app? Along with your "stellar" resume?

I hitch my leg up and lean on my knee, but he doesn't make me wait long. His answer comes quickly, like he doesn't have time for me.

Logan Carpino – No, my finger never slips in anything I do. Mistake, as in I didn't post my profile at all. Someone else did. Like I said, no hard feelings.

I ignore the finger comment.

Me – You're not single?

Logan Carpino – I'm very single.

Me – So you were hacked.

More bubbles dance on the screen, longer this time, and I wonder if he's writing a dissertation with a capital P.

Logan Carpino – Look, I don't know who you are, and you certainly don't know me. I work for a Fortune 500 company. Our transactions are not only lucrative, but highly sensitive. We have safeguards in place and take that very seriously. I most certainly was not hacked. The profile you swiped on was a joke posted by my brother and brother-in-law, who still act like they're in middle school. They've been fully chastised and disowned for it. As I said to begin with, a mistake. I don't have time for anyone and even less for dating apps.

I can't help it. A small smile spreads across my face.

Me – You don't think you can be hacked?

Logan Carpino – I know I can't be hacked.

27

Good luck with online dating, life, and all your future endeavors.

Now, my smile might as well break my face in two.

Me – Hmm. Say less.

Logan Carpino – What the hell does that mean?

I put my phone on silent and bring up the website for Andopolis Global. I have plenty of time to finish the assessment and write my report for my client. Right now, I want to have some fun.

It might be my poor luck with dating apps. Or the fact my last encounter ended with a fictional villain turning into a peeping Tom. Or the fact my dad had to step in and take care of that for me, and there's nothing I hate more than that.

I'm an adult with my very own fixer upper. There's nothing I want more than to be a mature, grown-ass woman who can take care of shit herself.

You'd think striving to be mature would be enough to stop me in my tracks. But I can't step away from a dare. Call it the *little sister syndrome* I've never been able to shake. I always want to keep up with my older, yet thoroughly irritating, brothers.

Plus, I know how to cover my tracks. And with what I'm about to do, I'm going to need to implement all my skills.

I might not have been the one to swipe Logan Carpino's profile, but he's the one who didn't like what he saw and started making shit up to get out of an awkward meet.

My fingers fly. Mr. VP with a capital P can go screw himself.

FOUR
LOGAN WITH A LOWERCASE P

Logan

I'm about to wrap up for the day.

Today was good.

I think we're at a turning point where those who used to be in middle management, but are now going to be trusted with running the company after we sell it, don't hate me as much as they did when I first stepped foot into their country.

And I haven't found any other buried apps on my phone with shitty profiles.

I'm calling it a win-win for the day.

Last night after I got home, I took the time to study my profile on Force of Nature—the one that resulted from Grant and Link drinking too much. I'm surprised I didn't throw my phone through the glass doors of my penthouse apartment when I saw it.

Not that any of it was a lie.

But what the fuck?

And Demetria Benjamin, the IT specialist from Winter Falls, actually swiped on it. Is she insane?

She must be. No self-respecting woman with half a brain would want anything to do with the man they made me look like.

Although, it really is me. Just not the me I'd ever advertise, let alone try to sell on a dating app.

If I ever used a dating app, which I haven't.

Crazy as she must be, Demetria was definitely a woman I'd look at twice if we passed on a city street. Long, dark hair, and athletic since her profile shows her favorite things to do are hike and shred the slopes on a snowboard.

Still, I don't have time for anyone. I travel over seventy percent of the time. Not to mention, I live in Manhattan and she lives on a mountain in the middle of nowhere. We couldn't be more different. Though, the woman must be into assholes, because that is exactly what my profile screams.

I checked every file and folder on my phone to make sure Grant and Link didn't do anything else while they made a trip back to middle school. Rugby must have distracted them, because, thank fuck, there was nothing else.

But I haven't deleted the damn app—yet. I almost did, but when it came down to it, something stopped me.

I'll do it tonight. I don't need anyone else swiping on my shit profile, even if it is the truth.

I'm about to shut my laptop and pack it away for the night, but something catches my eye. Or someone.

Lina.

She's running.

Or, trying to in her low heels.

And a look of panic is painted on her face as she rushes to my office.

I stand as she bursts through my office door. "What's wrong?"

"I... Logan—" she starts, but stutters, which isn't like her at all. Lina has no problem saying exactly what's on her mind. "I don't know how to tell you this. Something has happened. Something that you're not going to be happy about."

I frown and brace. "What is it?"

She bites her lip and glances down at her phone before looking back at me. "I'm sure you got it too. It's a global email. It went to the entire company. World-wide. And..."

I pick up my phone and open my email. "And?"

As my email downloads, her tone trails off. "And to most of our clients and acquisition holdings."

Her words barely have a chance to sink in when I see it. The subject line is telling enough. I sit my ass in my chair, and my stomach turns when I open the damn thing.

From: ;-)
To: Andopolis Global
Subject: Logan Carpino: A lowercase p
Logan Carpino is a failure when it comes to all things women. Also, he didn't think it was possible to be hacked.
He was wrong.

"What the fuck," I mutter and read it again. And again. And again.

"Um, corporate says we've been hacked."

I turn my glare on Lina. "You think?"

"They, ah, want to know what you might know

about this?" Her lips press into a fine line. "Since you're the subject."

"I don't know anything about this," I growl and look back at the email that has gone out to thousands of people. "And I'm not a failure when it comes to women, dammit!"

Her expression falls, and she takes a step back. "Oh … Okay. I can relay that to the team if you'd like."

"No. I'll take care of it." I squeeze my eyes shut and pinch the bridge of my nose. "I need to make some calls."

"Of course." She turns to the door before looking back. "Do you need anything before I go? We have tickets to the Opera, but I can cancel if you need me."

I shake my head and wave her off. "I can take care of it. Sorry … about biting your head off. And everything else. Enjoy your night."

"Really, I can stay—"

I shake my head. "No. Go. Someone obviously got into our system to get back at me for … whatever reason."

Lina could be something between my mother and a much older sister. She doesn't take shit from anyone, least of all me, and feels way too comfortable saying whatever she wants. "You know, if you're having problems in the *dating* department, I'd be happy to help."

I narrow my eyes. "I'm good, but thanks."

"My niece is single. You might like her—she works at a bakery."

"I don't need help in that department."

"My best friend back in New York has a son who's single if you prefer—"

"Really, Lina," I interrupt. "I don't need any help in any part of my life."

She hikes a brow. "The global email states otherwise."

I cannot believe this shit. "Go. I have to call my boss and I'm sure cybersecurity is going to want another meeting with me. They should all be getting to work on the other side of the world soon."

She's almost out the door when she turns to look at me one last time before leaving me to clean up the dumpster fire Grant and Link created. "Seriously, my niece is pretty—"

"Leave, or I'll rip up your Opera tickets."

"Good luck, Logan."

I look back to the damn email and dread the string of phone calls I'm about to make. I'm going to need more than luck.

Just when I'm about to bring up his contact, a notification pops up on my phone.

A fucking notification. Only the second one I've ever received.

But this time it's not the dating app, it's a text from an email address that's longer than I've ever seen.

Unknown – So, it seems your company and your cell can be hacked. Granted, it took me longer than normal.

Who in the hell is this woman?

Me – Who are you?

Unknown – No one you'd be interested in. We've already been over that.

Me – That wasn't what I meant, and you know it. That's beyond the point right now. What you did is illegal. You'll be in a shitload

of trouble when my company files charges. I know who you are.

Unknown – They won't be able to trace it back to me because I'm that good. And I got into your phone. You're one weird dude. Who turns off all notifications? No worries, I rectified that.

Hell. This woman has access to … everything.

Unknown – Check your email again.

I don't even have a chance to flip screens. A notification to said email pops up, and ironically, it's from *me*—my own fucking email address. I click on it, and pray she hasn't booby trapped my cell to remote detonate in my face.

There's an attachment, but I don't open it.

Unknown – Go on. Open the email. It's safe, I promise.

I look around my office. I feel violated. Like I'm in a Bourne movie and someone is watching me from across the Harbour.

I'm too curious, and it's only a phone. If it implodes, I'll buy a new one.

I click on the file.

It's a report.

A cybersecurity report.

I lean back in my chair and flip through the document. It's over one hundred pages. At the end, there are recommendations on how Andopolis Global can secure its servers and networks.

Another text notification pops up.

How does the world live like this? So fucking intrusive, but I guess not everyone has a Lina.

Unknown – I don't break into systems without fixing them. And no matter how high in the sky you live, I charge a lot for my services. Your company just got for free what I normally charge upwards of five figures for, simply because you're an asshole, and I wanted to prove your system could be hacked. You're welcome. Take that to your boss. It'll make up for the company-wide email. But that was fun.

Me – Wait. Demetria, right? Is that your real name?

Unknown – I guess you'll never know.

Me - This is nuts. How do I get hold of you?

Unknown – Dude.

Me – I haven't been on a skateboard in years —don't call me dude.

Unknown – Maybe you shouldn't take yourself so seriously and get back on a skateboard.

Me – I can't believe you hacked into my company.

Unknown – Of course you can't.

Me – And my phone.

Unknown – Gotta go, Logan with a lowercase p. I have work to do—real work for actual paying customers since I stayed up all night digging through your files. Also, you don't have an emergency contact listed with your company. My dad would frown upon that. Nice bonus package by the way.

What I want to tell her is I have a different package that's bigger and better, but that might be a poor first impression.

Or, worse. If that's possible.

Unknown – Have a nice life.

Me – Wait.

Unknown – Bye-bye.
Me – Demetria.
Me – Wait.
Me – Give me your number.
Me – Demetria!
Me – Call me. You obviously know how to get hold of me.

I toss the damn cell to the desk and lean back to stare at the ceiling. The woman just tore through my life like a tornado.

There's nothing I should be curious about.

I should be pissed.

I should file charges.

I always can, but there's no hurry. The evidence isn't going anywhere. Hell, I have it on my email and text thread. She admitted to hacking into my company and my personal phone.

It's still too early in the States to call my boss. While I wait, I pull up the damn dating app again.

Now I want to know everything about the woman who tried to humiliate me in front of my entire company and all of our clients.

Joke's on her. She caught my eye. Little does she know, I live my personal life like I do my professional one. When I want something, I'm relentless.

Persistent.

Some even call me ruthless.

Mediocre doesn't get you to where I am in life.

Demetria Benjamin...

You have my attention.

FIVE
PERFECT STORM

Demi

I guzzle another cup of coffee as I pay the price for my quick temper.

Hacking into a corporation like Andopolis Global without an official contract and full permission was stupid. In this case, my stupidity is so monumental, I could win a Darwin award.

But the Perfect Italian pissed me off.

I don't like people telling me I can't do things. Working in a male-dominated industry, I get it way too much. I have to give it to him, his company's networks are set up well, but that doesn't make them ironclad.

On the other hand, sliding into his cell was so easy, it might as well have been lubricated.

A banging comes from my front door, and Posey is peeking in through the glass squares. I trudge to the door, still in the pajamas I put on two days ago. Deadlines and unplanned hacking attempts really put a damper on daily showers.

When I open the door, cool air hits me, and so does her concern. "You look like shit."

"Thanks. I've been busy."

She makes herself at home, and I shut the door behind her. I watch her go straight to my kitchen and pour herself a cup of my afternoon pot of coffee. I'm pretty sure I need it more than she does at the moment. She's showered with a full face of makeup, and her hair is perfect. She's ready to take on the world.

I'm jealous.

She puts the mug to her lips. "We need to talk about what happened at the bar the other night."

I flop down on my sofa. "Yes. Let's talk about that. The guy you swiped on Force of Nature is real. A legit, real-life asshole. And I do not need another asshole in my life right now. I just got rid of the last one."

She sets her mug on the counter with a thunk. "Wait. That was a real profile?"

I shrug. "He said it was a mistake. But what he really meant was he wasn't into me, so he blamed someone else for posting his profile up without his knowledge. He's as transparent as my drafty windows. I asked if he'd been hacked and he said he couldn't be hacked—"

Posey interrupts me. "You didn't."

"You know I did."

A small smile creeps over her pretty face. "And?"

"And I proved him wrong. Personally and professionally. But it took me way too long, and I lost sleep doing it. That's why I look like shit."

"You're too smart for your own good."

"Whatever. It's done, and I can move on. And you

will never, ever touch my phone again. I blame this on you."

She ignores that. "What's he like?"

"He's a jerk who I'll never talk to again. Now, what did you come here to tell me about the other night at the bar?"

Another rap at my door interrupts us. Since Posey has actually slept in the last forty-eight hours, I don't move when she goes to answer it.

"I have a delivery for," the guy looks down at his tablet, "*Demetria-you-got-me-good-Benjamin*?"

I hop up so fast, I get a head rush. "Who is it from?"

"Says it's from Capital P." He looks up and shoves the enormous box at us. "Have a good day."

"Wait," I call for him. "Let me get you a tip."

"No need. Tip was paid by the sender. Enjoy!"

Posey shuts the door, and I lug the box to the middle of the room. We stare at it as if it's a ticking time bomb.

I don't look away from the mysterious delivery. I'm nervous. All I can think about is Sam. "I shouldn't have hacked this guy or his company. I have a feeling he's got resources far and wide. I mean, if he meets his goals, his bonus package is more money than I've made. Like, ever in my life."

"For real?"

I look over at her. "For real. The guy isn't just an ass, he's a loaded one. You really know how to pick 'em."

Her teeth sink into her bottom lip, and she finally shows a bit of remorse. Not that she hacked the guy. That's on me.

"We're opening it. I can't wait another second."

Posey grabs a pair of scissors off my desk and rips into the box. But we both freeze once she flips the top open and the contents come into view. "What the—"

I reach in and dig through the layers. "Holy shit."

"He must have studied your profile with a magnifying glass."

I hold up a package of red licorice. "I didn't say I like Twizzlers."

"Yes, but wasn't there a package sitting next to you on the table in one of your pictures? I'm pretty sure I took that one. And let's be real, you always have licorice laying around."

That's true. I pretty much can't make it through the day without reaching for my Twizzlers.

"Wow. Did he buy out Costco?"

"There's a note." Posey pushes my hand out of the way and reaches in. She rips the envelope open and her eyes widen.

I brace. "Shit. What does it say?"

Her gaze flits to mine. "Um, I don't know whether this is hot or disturbing."

"Dammit, Posey. What does it say?"

She doesn't read it aloud, so I rip the paper out of her hands.

Then my ass finds the sofa, because I can't support my own weight, and take in his message:

Demetria,
If you're reading this, that means you're not the only resourceful one.
Logan with a capital P

"I'm sorry." I glance up at Posey who looks

contrite. "I was just having fun. I didn't mean to attract another stalker. I feel horrible."

I shake my head. "Don't worry. For some reason, I don't get stalker vibes from this guy. Plus, when I hacked into his phone, it was in Australia. He's going to have to come a long way to be a stalker."

She crosses her arms and shifts her weight. "But he found where you live. And gloated about it."

I look back at the note. For some reason I'm almost relieved. Logan was right, both he and his company could come after me for hacking into their networks. Now that he's done this, it feels like we're even in some weird, demented way. "It's really okay. It's just licorice, right? It's not like he's sending me dead rabbits."

Posey looks at her watch. "Are you going to be okay? I have a deadline but was out for lemons for my throat. You were on the way so I thought I'd swing by."

I get up and give her a hug. "I'm good. And I really need to take a shower."

"If you're sure. Call me if you need anything. Seriously, if this guy goes dead rabbit on you, your dad will kill me."

I toss her a bag of Twizzlers. "My dad will never know about this. Trust me, I've seen Logan Carpino's calendar. He has no free time to be a stalker, no matter which hemisphere he's living in. His schedule is insane."

"I'll see you later. But I can be here with my pepper spray in no time. And not the regular stuff. I'll break out the big guns and bring the bear spray I carry when we hike."

"You must love me to break out the bear spray. I'll talk to you later."

She waves one more time on the way to her car.

I shut the door—and lock it—before ripping open a bag of Twizzlers. I'll never be able to eat all these before they go bad. Everyone's getting licorice for Christmas, because I have no qualms regifting.

I head up the stairs to take a shower, but see a flash of light on my phone. When I pick it up, there's a notification from Force of Nature. And since men can't approach women, my insides do a flip-flop, because it can only be from one person.

I slide my finger across, and Logan appears, flipping me off in all his beautiful Italian glory.

Logan – I hope you'll accept my apology for assuming I couldn't be hacked.

I stare at the screen as I make my way up the stairs to my room.

Logan – If the Twizzlers in the picture weren't yours, then I've got another awkward moment coming. Not as awkward as explaining to my boss about the email. That wasn't fun.

I climb onto my bed and curl up on my side.

Logan – But he did appreciate your detailed report. Our IT team is already busy making those patches.

I start to reply, but the man is relentless.

Logan – Do I need to send you more candy to get your attention?

Me – Wow. Demanding much?

Logan – Yes. All the time, in fact.

Me – I love Twizzlers, but in moderation. Not a decade's supply at one time.

Logan – Go big or go home. I needed your attention.

Me – Why?

Logan – Because you didn't call me. But now that I have your name, address, and phone number, you can't hide.

Me – You know, I just got rid of one stalker. I don't need another one.

Bubbles appear. And stop. And appear again.

Logan – You have a stalker?

Me – Had. So, not anymore. And hopefully never again.

Logan – I'm no stalker.

Me – You claim to have my address that I didn't give you.

Logan – Okay, I'm not usually a stalker. Do I need to remind you how you hacked into my company and my phone?

Me – You just thanked me for that.

Logan – I think we're even.

Me – Then what do you want?

Logan – I want to start over.

I pause.

Logan – Hello?

Me – I'm tired. I've been up forever working my day job and hacking into your shit. And I swore off dating. Specifically online dating.

Logan – But, you swiped me.

Me – Well, not exactly…

Logan – Shit. Yet another awkward moment to add to my list.

Me – My friend swiped on your profile. It was a joke.

Logan – So what you're saying is this is the perfect storm that never should have been. Interesting.

Me – I guess that's one way to put it.

My insides tighten, and I'm not sure why.

Logan – Demetria?

I pause, because everything about this stranger screams red flags.

Logan – Did I lose you, hacker?

Oh, no he didn't.

Me – You think you're funny.

Logan – I'm the least funny person you'll ever meet. Intense? Hell, yes. Funny? I don't have time to be funny.

Me – For someone with so little time, you sure are wasting it on a dating app you never intended to be on in the first place. You're the one who called this the perfect storm.

Logan - A quagmire.

Me – A comedy of errors?

Logan – Definitely a train wreck.

Me – A clusterfuck.

Logan – Now you're turning me on.

I bite back a smile.

Me – I've got to go.

Logan – I'm going to call you later, and you're going to answer.

Me – Now you're FUBAR.

Logan – Exactly. Looking forward to hearing your voice for the first time, Demetria.

Me – Everyone calls me Demi.

Logan – Demi. Answer your phone.

Me – If I do, the bar is set high. Your profile promises perfection with a capital P. I want you to know that I refuse to settle for anything less.

Logan – What my fucking brother should've

added to my profile is that I'm as confident as I am determined. You just laid a challenge at my feet, Demi, and I never back down from a challenge.

Me – If you say so. Just think of the global emails if you fail.

Logan – Well played, hacker.

Me – Gotta go. I have a meeting and need to shower first.

Logan – I haven't even heard your voice yet and now I'm thinking of you in the shower. Online dating is shit. I don't know how normal people do this.

Me – You're something.

Logan – Trust me, I'm everything.

Me – Goodbye, Logan Carpino.

Logan – Answer your phone when I call.

I'm afraid he won't stop, so I toss my phone to my other pillow and shut my eyes. I wasn't kidding. I want to take a break. I *need* to take a break. Christmas will be here in a blink, and I don't need some stranger stringing me along, or worse, not taking no for an answer. Because both have happened in the last few months.

I'm tired.

And none of this puts me in the Christmas spirit.

SIX
DELETE

Logan

I haven't called Demi yet. Being on opposite sides of the globe proves to be a roadblock when it comes to online dating. She said she needed to work and was tired. But the sun will be rising in North America soon—it'll be time to make my move.

As an adult, I'm used to women falling at my feet. The more successful I've become, the more it happens.

It wasn't always that way. No one was throwing themselves at my feet when I was young, skinny, and the Quiz Bowl champion.

I can thank the Quiz Bowl team for my scholarships, high test scores, and stellar IQ, but I have to thank the gym for my thirty pounds of muscle. I might've been the smartest in my family, but I was downright scrawny.

Apparently muscle attracts females more than high-functioning brain cells. In the beginning, I enjoyed it. I also took advantage when I was in the mood.

Then, I got bored.

Who am I kidding? I'm still bored.

But I think I've had a moment of self-realization.

An awakening. An epiphany of sorts.

No one has ever challenged me.

Sure, at work they do all the time. But in my personal life?

Never.

I pissed off Demetria Benjamin, and she fucking hacked into my company's servers and sent an embarrassing email, if for no other reason than to humiliate me, because she thought I wasn't interested in her. Then she hacked into my phone. But the woman has a conscience, giving us a detailed plan on what we needed to do so no one else could penetrate our business and do anything worse.

I studied her profile on Force of Nature. I actually created a fucking Instagram account just so I could see her profile and study every picture she's posted since high school. There was even less on Facebook, so I deleted that account faster than I created it, thank fuck.

Then I googled her. There wasn't much there, other than she's the daughter of the county sheriff.

"Hey, Lina. What do you know about Winter Falls?"

She looks up from her laptop. "We used to take the kids skiing there when they were young. It's a quaint little mountain town at the base of the slopes. You thinking about a vacation over Christmas?"

I anchor the toe of my Italian loafer beneath me and swivel back and forth in my chair as I look out at the water. I've been distracted for most of the day and I'm never distracted. "I think I might."

"After Christmas though, right? Tia Carpino will not be happy if you're not at her table on Christmas day. I don't want to think about the repercussions."

Christmas is next week. Lina and her husband are going back to the States tomorrow. I need to be here for a couple of meetings and will be cutting it close to make it home for the big day. But she's right. It doesn't matter how old I am or how successful I've become. My mom will be pissed if I'm not there.

"Does this have anything to do with your online love interest?"

I narrow my eyes. "I don't have a love interest, online or otherwise."

She nods slowly. "Okay. I can read between the lines. That email screamed *scorned lover*, if I ever saw it."

I glare before standing and grab my basketball off the credenza, twirling it on my finger as I stare out the windows. "There's nothing to be scorned over. It was a *misunderstanding*."

"I don't think someone hacking into Andopolis Global networks says misunderstanding. There are emotions behind something like that."

I turn to look at her and am about to argue, but she keeps talking.

"I've worked with you for a long time, Logan. I might be your assistant, but I'm also a mom. I think someone finally stood up to you and got your attention. If I had to guess, you might even like it."

I dribble the ball back and forth, but don't answer. She's right. Then again, Lina usually is because she's the best. And I never hesitate in telling her that, but we're also not usually talking about my private life.

There's no way I'm confirming that shit.

"Let me guess. You don't have a hankering to hit the slopes, but the hacker lives in Winter Falls?"

My lips press into a thin line before I give her a warning that I'm sure she'll laugh at. "Watch it. I haven't given you your Christmas present yet."

She rolls her eyes and looks pretty damn confident that I'm blowing smoke. Who am I kidding? I'd never do that. Anyway, I am beyond the cancellation date for a house on St. Thomas. Her kids are in college and she worries about wet T-shirt contests and beer bongs. I'm giving her control over her kids.

And I get a happy Lina.

Win-win.

Though Lina on vacation might as well be hell week for me.

"Do me a favor, don't miss your flight and spend Christmas alone Down Under. You shouldn't have pushed your trip so late in the month. I know you, and you'll end up working straight through."

I turn back to the window. "The flight is hell. I don't know why I'm bothering. Christmas on the beach doesn't sound too bad."

"Don't you dare. Do I have to stay and fly back with you to make sure you make it to Omaha?"

I return to spinning the basketball, but on my middle finger this time and grin. "Goodbye and merry Christmas."

She narrows her eyes on me and shakes her head. "You need something to shake up your life. Something unexpected. A change of perspective that will knock you on your ass. That's my Christmas wish for you, Logan Carpino."

"I thought we were friends. Who wishes that shit on someone? That's more like a hex. Now I'm definitely returning your gift," I lie.

She levels her gaze and her index finger on me. "Check your phone. I'll be checking in and I expect you to answer."

"Who works for who, here?"

"Who works for *whom*," she corrects.

"I know it's *whom*, but *who* talks like that?"

She ignores me and slings her bag up to her shoulder. "You need me and you know it. I'll see you next year. Have fun in Nebraska."

"I'll be jolly as fuck," I mutter and drop the ball to the credenza behind my desk. I go straight to my cell and hit go on the newest contact in my phone: Hacker.

Just when I think she's going to ignore me and not answer, she picks up, but doesn't even greet me with a *hello*. "Do you always follow through?"

I pause, taking in her voice for the first time. It's light and smooth and has a hint of a smile. "Good morning, Demi. Yes. Something to know about me, I don't make idle threats. Do you always hack into people's phones?"

"Only when I'm trying to figure out if a profile on a dating app is real or if someone is punking me. I don't like to be punked."

I lean back in my chair and prop my feet up on my desk. "You sound different than I imagined."

"Really?" Her words flow smoothly through the line—her tone thoroughly feminine and way too easy on my ears. "What did you imagine I'd sound like?

"You're a hacker. Before this week, I assumed

hackers holed up in their parents' basements, throwing back Red Bulls while chain smoking."

"Sorry to disappoint you. I like fresh, mountain air, and coffee is my only vice. If you're looking for something else, you should update your profile."

"I deleted my profile this afternoon. You need to delete yours too."

It sounds like she's banging around a kitchen as she speaks. "Why should I delete my profile?"

I open a file on my laptop. A screenshot of Demetria Benjamin pops up that I took before I deleted the app. She's hiking. Her dark hair is piled high on her head, she's makeup free, and her toned, athletic body is on display. I barely even notice the perfect mountain range in the backdrop—that's how stunning she is. "You're the one who said you were done with online dating. Plus, you've met me. I promise, everyone else will fail in comparison."

"Wow."

"I know. I'm sorry about that. Knowing me will ruin the rest of the male species for you."

"Cocky much?"

"All the time. You'll learn to appreciate it."

"I'm not sure about that…"

"I like the sound of your voice."

She pauses before admitting, "I'm not sure what to think about you."

"Why?"

"I told you. I just had a weird situation from my last online dating experience. I wasn't kidding when I said I was done. Then a lifetime supply of Twizzlers shows up on my doorstep, a doorstep I didn't give an address for. Sorry if I have cold feet."

I stare at the screenshot one more time that makes

me feel a little bit like a stalker, so I close the file. "What can I do to convince you I'm not a stalker?"

"See, that's the thing." She sighs, and the banging stops, making me wonder if she's maybe settled with a cup of her favorite vice. I open my browser and search coffee gift baskets as she goes on. "I don't think you're a stalker. At least you don't feel like one. I honestly don't know when you'd have the time."

I click on the biggest package with the quickest delivery. With a rush fee almost as expensive as the gift itself, it'll be there tomorrow. "How do you know how I spend my time?"

"Logan, I don't even think you have any hobbies. I've seen your calendar and read your emails. By the looks of your online activity, you even work on the weekends."

"You know, I should be pissed about that. And I have hobbies."

"Really? Like watching golf? That's not a hobby."

"I play too." I try to think about the last time I picked up my clubs. It's been so long, I can't even remember.

"It takes at least a half a day to play golf. You haven't taken that much of a break from emails or meetings for the last two months. I got too tired to look back any further. Your schedule is just that boring."

"Says the woman who stayed up all night to hack into my company just to prove me wrong. And don't try to claim hacking is a hobby. Doesn't count if you get paid for it."

I can tell I got her there. She has no comeback.

I press purchase on the gift basket and shut my laptop. "Here's the thing. I'm busy. More than busy. And you're right, I have no time for hobbies right now.

I travel eight and a half months out of the year. I haven't made time for anyone or anything else in a long time."

"You're a walking billboard for the Force of Nature app," she deadpans.

"I know," I agree. "It's bad."

"At least you admit it."

"But for the first time in a long time, someone caught my attention."

That shuts her up.

"I want to meet you, Demi. In person."

"I, umm... I don't know."

"What are you doing after Christmas?"

"Nothing. Probably just working. The slopes are way too busy at Christmas. But aren't you halfway around the world?"

"I've decided I'm not going to allow it to bother me that you know every nuance of my life."

I hear a smile in her smooth voice. "Sorry."

"Somehow I doubt you are. In case you haven't had time to dig into my travel plans, I'm leaving tomorrow to fly home for the holidays. After Christmas, maybe I'll hit up the mountains."

"You'd come all this way just to meet me?"

"Hacker, when I say no one has interested me in a long time, I'm not exaggerating. At this point, I can't move on and forget about you."

"I guess..."

"If it turns out you have a shitty personality, I'll make a snow angel, hop the next flight for the southern hemisphere, and we'll both pretend we didn't accidentally meet on the internet. How does that sound?"

"It sounds like it could be a Hallmark movie ... or a *Dateline* special. But definitely nothing in between."

"Since I don't do anything half-assed, that sounds about right."

She hums her agreement, and I can't help it. I like the sound. And my dick does too—he twitches with curiosity.

"I've got to go. I have a company just begging me to hack into their networks."

"I'm not surprised. As good as you are, I bet you get a lot of people begging. I might be one of them someday. You know, after Christmas."

"Thanks for the licorice, Logan. I'll send you my dental bill if I end up with cavities."

"Thank you for answering. You had me wondering there for a few rings. And, Demi?"

"Yeah?"

"Delete your profile."

Another laugh hits me, and this time it's a little darker. Like a dare. "I'll think about it."

"Have a good day, hacker."

"Bye, Logan."

She hangs up, and I do a quarter spin in my chair. The sun is setting over the Harbour. I leave soon to make the flight back to the States. I'll book another flight and hotel in Winter Falls the day after Christmas.

For the first time in a very long time—so long, I can't even remember the last time it happened—I'm actually excited to meet someone.

Until then, I have work to wrap up before the holiday. I'll be gone until the new year.

A lot can happen in that time.

SEVEN

SCRATCH THE ITCH

Demi

"*What is normally a white Christmas here in Winter Falls could turn whiter. If you like to hit the slopes over the holidays, this might be your year. There are two systems headed our way, and that means fresh powder for the mountains…*"

"Your dad has to work Christmas," my mom explains over the phone as I wrap presents with the TV keeping me company in the background. "We'll have a small dinner on the day, but I'm doing a big get together the day after."

I freeze in the middle of tying a bow. "Mom, I have plans that day."

"What do you mean, you have plans? It's Christmas!"

"No, the day after. I have plans."

"With whom?"

"I have a date." I don't explain further, because the

incident with Sam was enough for my parents. I think I'd rather walk through a blizzard barefoot before telling them I met someone else online.

"With whom?" she demands.

"A guy." I think for a hot second. "Posey set me up with him."

"I don't know if that's good or not. Who is it?"

"His name is Logan. It's no one you know. He doesn't live here."

"I don't know, Demi. After what happened last time—"

"Mom, not everyone is a stalker. I did my research. He seems … normal."

Normal is the wrong word to attach to Logan Carpino. From what I can tell, there's nothing normal about the man.

All of sudden she perks up. "Bring him to dinner! That way your dad can do his thing."

"I haven't met him in person yet, and you want me to bring him to a major family holiday? You're crazy."

"No, Sam Valder-what's-his-face was crazy. I am a concerned parent."

"Even so, there's no way in hell I'm bringing him to a Christmas dinner."

"Well." She exhales loudly enough to be heard on the next peak. "I don't know why you have to be so hard headed."

"Gotta go, Mom. I have presents to finish wrapping. I'll see you tomorrow."

"Wait, you saw the weather? We're supposed to get a lot of snow. Are you prepared, just in case?"

"Finally. We need some fresh powder." I grab another package of Twizzlers to wrap. "There's a knock on my door. Gotta go. Love you."

"Whatever, you're ruining Christmas for a blind date."

"Seriously," I mutter. "Talk to you tomorrow."

I hang up before she manages to dump another layer of guilt on me and climb to my feet. When I open the door, the wind is blowing a fury and someone is standing in front of me holding an enormous basket covered in cellophane. It's exploding with mugs, cookies, bags of coffee, and I think I even see a French press.

"Can I help you?" I ask.

"Demetria Benjamin?"

"That's me."

"Here." He shoves the basket my way, and it's so heavy, I have to turn and set it on the floor. That's when I see the same delivery guy who brought me the Twizzlers. "Sorry it's so late. That was a rush order and they insisted it had to be delivered tonight."

I look down at the basket and pluck the card off the top. Before I open it, I turn back to the delivery guy. "Was the tip included again?"

He stuffs his gloved hands into his pockets. "Sure was. I'll deliver all night if the tips keep coming in like that."

I smile. "I appreciate you driving out here this late. Merry Christmas."

His teeth chatter. "Merry Christmas."

I shut the cold out and pull my thick cardigan around my middle. I guess we are going to get some weather with the way that wind is whipping.

I open the envelope and it's typed out on the same thick cardstock the Twizzlers came with.

Something to keep you warm until we meet.

I can't help but smile. I wonder if his note is as basic as the words typed on it.

Or if he means something else entirely.

Because I can't help thinking of other ways to stay warm after we meet, which is ridiculous. I've had one conversation with the man, a few exchanges on text, and another through a dating app.

I mean, I feel like I know everything about him. I combed through his pictures, contacts, and text messages. His emails were boring as hell—all numbers, profits, losses, and other mumbo jumbo that means nothing to me. I put two and two together that his younger sister is a GRAMMY award-winning songwriter in Nashville. And there are enough Carpinos in his contacts to make up their own phone book thick enough to be used as a stepstool.

But most importantly, he had no text strings with women who weren't Carpinos or work associates. And I scrolled and scrolled and scrolled.

Nada.

Which makes me believe he's too busy to be a stalker or a player. Not being a stalker doesn't surprise me. The man is hot. He has no need to be a stalker. I'm sure women throw themselves at his feet at every opportunity.

But the player part?

Again, he's hot. He could play every field, court, or rink of any sport, and my guess, most women wouldn't care.

I mean, I would care. If I had someone like him, I wouldn't share either.

Which is probably why my mind went to him keeping me warm.

I should not know this much about a man whom I've communicated with so little.

Shit. Maybe I'm the stalker.

I'm just about to pull the ribbon to see what he sent me when another rap at my door startles me. It can't be another delivery.

I'm about to turn and reach for the handle, but I hear a quick click and it shifts on its own.

I don't have enough time to reach for the bolt when the cold air flows into my house.

"Demi, long time no see."

Logan's card flits to the floor as I put a hand to his chest to stop him from moving in farther. "Sam! What the hell are you doing?"

"It's cold, and the door was unlocked. I saw your light on. Can I come in and warm up?"

"Are you serious? No! You shouldn't be here."

"I wanted to bring you something. You know, for Christmas. I thought maybe this would be a good time to talk about what happened."

"There's nothing to talk about. You know where I stand. I told you. My dad told you. And half the town told you when you wouldn't stop asking around about me."

"Look, I might've come on a little strong."

What the hell is wrong with this guy? "A little strong? You were lurking around my house and looking into my windows! I told you I didn't want to see you again, and you refused to leave. And now you're back, even after my father had to tell you to stay away—"

"About that." He tries to reach for me, but I swat his hand away. "Honey, please. Let me explain—"

He did not just *honey* me. Gross. But he doesn't have a chance to explain, because my phone interrupts. "Don't you dare take a step farther in my house." I reach over the enormous gift basket and grab my phone from the floor. I press go before looking to see who it is. "Hello?"

"Just wanted to make sure you got the coffee. You did say it's your only vice—"

"Yes," I snap as I stare at Sam. "It was just delivered. It's amazing, thank you. And for taking care of the tip."

"I don't know you well, but it doesn't sound as if you like it," Logan drawls.

"Who's that?" Sam demands.

"Who's that?" Logan echoes. I feel like I'm in a stereo from hell.

I keep my glare on Sam as I speak to Logan. "It's the guy I told you about the other day. The persistent one. You know? The stalker."

Sam lowers his voice. "Fuck that. I'm no stalker, Demi. I just want to talk to you."

"Are you alone with him?" Logan grits. A chill runs down my spine, and it has nothing to do with the frigid wind, but everything to do with Logan's tone. I might know everything about the man that hacking into his cell has to offer, but this side of someone is impossible to learn from reading their personal texts.

"Yes. I don't want to be alone with him, but he won't leave."

"Don't hang up, Demi. I'm going to make a call on the other line. Give me thirty seconds, but stay with me."

Sam takes another step inside the door. "Who are you talking to?"

I do my best to steady my tone. "That's none of your business."

"Stay on the line," Logan growls in my ear before the sound over the phone is muffled. He's talking, but not to me.

Sam tries to move in, but I hold my ground so he can't step in farther or shut it behind him. He pulls in a big breath and forces his jaw to go slack. "We ended on a bad note. I came on too strong. I get that now. I only want to talk, Demi. Give me five minutes to talk."

"We ended exactly the way we needed to end, as far as I'm concerned. You're clingy, demanding, and we have nothing in common. You were grumpy when I wanted to read and you don't like pizza. Hell, you didn't even slow down for chipmunks running across the road. Who doesn't like chipmunks? I don't need that kind of negativity in my life."

"I don't *not* like pizza," he claims. "I'm lactose intolerant."

"Demetria?" Logan calls for me.

"What?" I snap.

"The only thing better than extra cheese on a pizza is sex." Of all the pictures I found of Logan on the internet, he wasn't smiling in many of them. But right now, as he describes his love for dairy, I'm pretty sure he's as jolly as old Saint Nick. "And I'd be willing to do some questionable shit that borderlines illegal for an ice cream cake."

"Oh, for fuck's sake," I mutter.

"Get off the phone so we can talk," Sam demands again and puts a hand to my hip and pushes.

I smack him in the chest, and my foot connects with his shin.

"Ouch," Sam snaps.

That wipes the jolly right out of Logan's voice. "You okay?"

I try to keep my tone steady, but it's hard. "I'm fine, but he won't leave."

"Stay with me, Demi," Logan sooths. "I called Winter Falls' Sheriff's Department. Someone should be there soon."

My breath catches. "You did what?"

"What?" Sam echoes.

"I had no choice, baby. I'm in Sydney, half a world away from you. Hell, even if I were in New York, I'd be useless. Dammit. You've got an asshole on your doorstep, I'm calling someone to help you. When I explained the situation, they assured me you'd be a priority."

I groan internally. "I'm sure they did."

That's when it happens. I hear them before I see them. Sure, it's Christmas. In any Hallmark made-for-TV movie, there would be sleigh bells and the sounds of hoofs on freshly fallen snow. But not when it comes to me. Instead of a chivalrous knight in shining armor, I get sirens bouncing off the mountains through the dark, cold night. When flashing lights come into view as two cruisers round the corner on what seems like two wheels, Sam finally takes steps out onto my porch and hisses, "Fuck."

"I told you to leave," I complain. "But you wouldn't listen, just like before."

"They're there?" Logan asks.

"Yes. They're here."

Logan exhales a sigh of relief, and for some reason, it feels like a thick, gooey mug of hot chocolate on this otherwise dreary, frigid night.

Chocolate as dark as his eyes.

But that's beside the point.

"You called your dad?" Sam complains.

"No, I didn't call anyone. My…" I pause because I have no idea what Logan is to me besides my own personal hot Santa from Oz, who sends thoughtful gifts and makes me think dirty thoughts. I shrug as I struggle for words. "Someone … someone called for me."

"*Someone* who isn't lactose intolerant. I reserve the right to be clingy and demanding, though. We'll see how we hit it off when I get there."

My teeth sink into the tender skin of my lip because this is not an appropriate time to think of Logan being demanding in any way, let alone the good ways. I'm not sure what would be more inappropriate as my father climbs out of his SUV, the cruiser lighting up my mountain like a crime scene. I think the only thing worse would be imagining the stranger that is Logan Carpino going *down under* in a whole other way that has nothing to do with kangaroos or koala bears.

"Demi!" my father yells as he takes the steps up to my front door with one of his deputies trailing him. "You okay?"

I don't have the chance to nod when Sam steps in front of me and puts a hand up to my dad. "Sheriff Benjamin, calm down."

Oh shit.

Well, that wiped the smile off my face.

My father doesn't afford me a glance. His rage is off the charts and focused on the idiot standing between us. He grabs Sam by the bicep and flings him around. The man who just won't take no for an answer, has the side of his face smashed up against the stacked stone of my front porch.

Sam moans, "Let me explain—"

My dad snarls, "You have the right to remain silent."

Logan pipes in, "I hope I never get on your bad side."

"Mm-hmm."

"Demi," Sam begs. "Tell him we were just talking."

My dad's gaze darts to me, and I give my head a small shake.

Handcuffs circle Sam's wrists. Their click-click and my father informing him of his right to representation seals the deal.

Sam glares at me. "This is crazy. I haven't done shit to you."

"In my town, when a woman tells you to leave, you leave. You sure as fuck don't come back and sneak around her house or barge in her front door uninvited. You were warned, you ignored it, and now we're making it official."

"What are you arresting me for?"

"Trespassing. You know what? Let's make that criminal trespassing. And disorderly conduct since you've been belligerent, and I have a witness. Keep acting up, and we'll add to the list." Dad turns to the deputy and hands Sam off. "Get him back to the department and start processing him. I'll be right there."

Sam's grumbles trail off into the darkness, and my dad steps in front of me. "You're okay?"

I nod and sigh, still connected to the strange man who doesn't seem like a stranger anymore but is all the way around the world and still managed to help me. "I'm good, Dad."

"You still on the phone with the guy who called this in?"

"That would be me. You're welcome." Logan sounds proud of himself.

"I'll be calling him." Dad leans in and kisses my forehead. "Lock up. I'll call you later."

I give him a small wave. "Love you."

Logan interjects himself again. "Feels early for declarations of love, but I appreciate it nonetheless."

"Logan Carpino," I start as I shut my door, turning both the lock and deadbolt. "Who the hell are you? You'd think after going through your phone, I'd have you figured out, but I'm left clueless."

I hear him move as he speaks. "I don't date, Demi."

I stop going through the gift basket that contains enough coffee to outlast my supply of Twizzlers. "Sorry? I must have misunderstood you. You know, about meeting. If you think I'm only in this for a hookup—"

"That's not what I meant."

I exhale and fall back on the sofa. "You know, this might be a bad idea. I appreciate what you did tonight. Really, I do. But I'm mentally exhausted from dealing with Sam as it is. We're not even on the same continent—"

"We will be in a couple of days," he argues.

"But even when you're not traveling, we don't live near each other. And you just admitted that you don't date. I appreciate the candy and caffeine, but there's nothing about this that will work."

"Stop right there. I said I don't date because I don't have time. I also haven't made the time by choice. I've worked night and day for years to get where I am.

There's no other way to make it to the top without working myself to the bone to prove I can do what others have taken decades to do. I made it a priority, but it didn't come without compromise, Demi. I gave up a life outside of work."

I open a package of cookies and shove one in my mouth. The chocolate chunks melt on my tongue and it's as sweet as his story is depressing. Depressing and familiar.

But I don't admit that. "You really do look like you could use some balance from what I learned by creeping through your phone."

"At least I don't have to convince you I'm boring as hell."

"There's a chance you're not the only boring person on this call, Logan," I whisper.

His sigh is masculine and deep, and I wonder if he just laid down. "Demi?"

"Yeah?"

"I think you're curious. I know I'm more than curious. I don't believe in anything that isn't supported by cold, hard numbers. It's how I'm wired. But you entered my life with a force that's hard to ignore. I don't know you like you know me since the only hacking I've ever done was breaking the lock on my cousin's journal with her younger brother when we were kids. You're hot and gorgeous, and I'm sure you get a shitload of attention for your blue eyes and long legs alone, but it was your brain that stopped me in my tracks. Do me a favor and don't fuck this up. I'm anxious to scratch the itch of my curiosity."

I almost choke on my cookie. "You like my brain?"

"I didn't say that." His low tenor falls into sarcastic tone, somewhere on the scale between sexy and asshole. "I said it stopped me in my tracks. You think a lot of yourself."

I smile at the bag of cookies that will probably be my dinner. "You're the one who claims to be smarter than ninety-nine percent of the population, Mr. Wharton MBA."

"As true as that is, I didn't write it." He pauses and lowers his voice. "You okay? From that asshole pushing his way into your house?"

I put my cookies down and hug a toss pillow. "Yeah, I'm okay. My father will take care of it. It doesn't make me happy that he has to, but I know he will."

"Good. My travel agent had to jump through a shit ton of hoops, but I have a room reserved."

"I'm surprised. The lodge is usually booked between the holidays."

"Someone cancelled."

"We're supposed to get a lot of snow. I hope it doesn't get too bad."

"Nothing will keep me away. My determination isn't something you can learn from reading my private files."

"I don't know." It's my turn to crank up the sarcasm. "You were pretty cut-throat with that business deal last month. Pretty sure your persistence bled from those emails."

"Persistence…" He lets that word hang on his tongue.

"I have a year's worth of Twizzlers and coffee to show for it."

"Soon." His tone is lower this time, and his words seep through the phone and warm me in places that haven't felt emotion in a very long time. "Can't wait to lay eyes on you in the flesh. This online shit is for pussies—and not the good kind."

I can't help but laugh. "Safe travels, Logan Carpino."

"Drink your coffee, hacker. You're going to need it."

"You really don't know how to make me feel better about meeting someone online, do you?"

"Like I said, perfect storm. It's what happens when two forces collide and their energy becomes one," he explains. "I've got to finish packing. Keep in touch. I'm headed to the airport in an hour."

"I have to finish wrapping presents before it gets too late. Don't forget your underwear, Logan."

"I might like going commando," he teases. I cannot imagine him commando in his pricey suits.

"Goodnight," I offer to get us back on solid ground. I really don't want to discuss Logan not wearing underwear.

"Sweet dreams, Demetria."

I stuff another cookie in my mouth. Tomorrow is Christmas Eve. It's time to eat, drink, and be merry, right?

As the wind whirls around my home in an angry snarl, I finish wrapping presents and make a grocery list for what little I'm contributing to Christmas dinner by the warm lights of my small tree.

EIGHT
CATASTROPHIC

Logan

We finally touch down on American soil. It's a long-ass flight, and even though it was first class and I had a bed, I'm still stiff as hell and dehydrated. Fifteen hours in the air will do that to you.

It's Christmas Eve and I haven't seen my family since before I left for Australia. That is, other than the Grant and Link vacation that resulted in my first dating app experience, which led to me getting hacked, and making plans with a woman for the first time in years.

I can't let them know this. I'll never live it down.

I had no other choice than to travel on Christmas Eve. There were meetings I needed to be at yesterday, things that needed to be wrapped before the holiday and my extended break, and the flight practically takes a whole day. I might be in the States for a while, but I'll be working for most of it. I can't remember the last time I took a real vacation. Probably spring break my senior year in college. I assume it was fun since I don't remember much of it.

The concourse is packed with holiday travelers. My connecting flight to Omaha is on time, if I don't hurry, they'll shut the door on my ass, and my mom will have a Christmas fit.

But something catches my eye and I come to a stop at the entrance to a bar with TVs lining the wall. It's not the NFL playoffs that grab my attention, rather a colorful map.

A map of the mountain range with Winter Falls smack in the middle.

"Can you turn that up?" I ask the bartender.

He lifts his chin and grabs the remote. "Looks bad."

Bad is an understatement. Snow on a radar is usually white. Maybe pink if there's some ice.

But black?

"*...our analysis models did not see this coming. Either storm on their own would be a healthy dose of powder for Winter Falls. But the two converging like this could be catastrophic. I suggest residents in this area prepare to hunker down for a while and be ready in case you lose power. This winter system will turn into a blizzard and will sit over this area for days...*"

"Hope that's not where you're headed," the bartender adds. "Doubt you'll make it for Christmas."

My phone vibrates in my pocket and I don't look to see who it is when I answer. "Carpino."

"Logan."

I turn away from the bar and continue down the concourse. "Hacker. How are you?"

She sighs. "I'm afraid we'll need to reschedule. There's a storm coming, and it's bad. It's not safe to travel, you'll never make it."

"You don't say?"

"I know," she goes on. "I'm sorry. We get snowstorms in the mountains, but this is worse. This looks like it could be bad."

"I'm not cancelling yet. Maybe it won't be as bad as they say."

"It looks pretty bad. We haven't seen a storm like this in years."

"I've got to catch my connecting flight. I'll call you when I land again. But, Demi, this is happening."

"It's not like I'm cancelling on you. It's Mother Nature who's not cooperating. With the shift, it's heading here faster than they predicted."

"I'll call you. There's not much that gets in my way when I want something."

"Yes, the almighty Logan Carpino takes on blizzards." A tone dances in her words that's a balance of sarcasm and shit-giving. "Not going to happen. We'll have to plan on next year—if we ever get to meet in person."

I stop in my tracks and hitch my backpack up my shoulder. I look at my watch and when I don't answer, she calls out for me.

"Did I lose you?"

"No, I'm here. Look, I've got to go. Call you when I land."

She exhales, and I think I hear disappointment. "Have a safe flight."

"We'll talk soon, Demi."

I hang up, start to jog through the crowds, and think about how much easier this would be in Australia where the sun is shining and snowstorms aren't a thing at the holidays.

NINE

IRRATIONAL AND UNJUSTIFIED AND COMPLETELY SENSELESS

Demi

"This blizzard is ruining Christmas," my mother cries. She literally cries, blowing her nose over the phone as she laments the first Christmas she'll spend away from me. "Will you be okay? You won't be here for my beef tenderloin or bread pudding. Do you even have any food in the house? I told you to prepare."

"Yes, Mom. I have food. I'm an adult and I'll be fine."

"This could last days. Days!"

"Mom, settle down."

"At least your dad stocked your wood pile in case the power goes out. Goodness, I hope the power doesn't go out. The last time that happened, I put everything from the freezer in the snow and then it snowed some more, and I couldn't find anything for days."

"I'll be fine. I have a book and plenty of coffee," I

trail off and don't add that no one will die from a lack of sugar with my stash of Twizzlers.

"Please don't work. It's Christmas. You work too much as it is. We'll video chat often so you don't get lonely."

Internally, I cringe from the promise of frequent video chats. "Sounds good. Merry Christmas Eve. Love you."

"I'll call later. Maybe at midnight! To wish you a Merry Christmas."

"Whatever you want, Mom."

"Love you, Demi bug." Her tone turns desolate again before she disconnects.

I grab the remote to change the channel. The wind howls. I can't even see across my driveway, let alone the peaks of Winter Falls. It's snowing sideways and the lane leading to my house is already packed with snow. At this rate, the plows won't be able to do their thing until the visibility clears. And the way the forecast has changed, I doubt we'll see one for days.

I stoke my fire when the lights flicker.

"Shit," I hiss to no one, but my Christmas tree lights up again, and I breathe a sigh of relief. I wasn't kidding when I said to my mom I didn't mind being by myself, but I really don't want to be stuck without power.

I have the oven preheating for my pizza rolls, since I'm fancy like that, when it happens again.

The lights flicker.

Off.

On.

Off.

I pull in a breath.

On.

I exhale.

And, then … off.

I wait.

Nothing.

"Dammit."

I'm draped in darkness, the kitchen lit only by the falling snow outside. I could live in Winter Falls for a thousand years and forever be mesmerized how the snow lights up the house at night.

Even if it is snowing sideways.

I rummage through a junk drawer until I find my lighter. Who knows how long the power will be out, so I only light a couple of candles before stoking the fire. I'm about to go get another sweater to layer on when I hear a crash through the wind.

When I get to my front window, I pull back my shades and gasp. A car too small and not equipped for this weather is wrapped around the base of the enormous Douglas Fir next to my drive. Smoke is pouring from beneath the hood, and just like my house, its headlights flicker right before turning dark.

I step into my snow boots, but don't take the time to grab my coat, before flying out my front door. Shit, it's coming down hard. There's well over a foot of new snow as I trudge through my yard, leaning to cut through the wind.

The driver's door pushes open with metal-on-metal scratching when I yell, "Are you okay?"

Dark, thick hair, stark against our white surroundings, comes into view. Followed by a black jacket—not a coat—that looks more like a shirt. The man gets taller and taller as he stands, and the blizzard biting at my skin has nothing to do with the oxygen disintegrating from my lungs.

He turns.

What the hell?

He pauses when he sees me.

Logan Carpino is here?

And all I see are deep brown eyes, the angry ones that stared me down when I first opened his profile picture and he was flipping me off.

But they're not angry tonight.

"You're here?" My words are as idiotic as my thoughts, because he's clearly here, and just wrapped a car around a tree.

He says nothing, but reaches in the car before slamming the door, which really doesn't close since the entire thing is crushed.

I trudge forward as fast as I can and meet him on the other side of the tree. He swings a backpack over his shoulder and lifts a hand to his forehead. He's bleeding at the temple.

I get my first good look at him through the storm, blood and all. He's everything his profile promised and more. Tall and broad, dark eyes, thick, wavy hair, and even a hint of sun.

He did come all the way from Australia while the rest of us here in America have been holed away in the cold. He's a workaholic—maybe he brings his laptop to the beach on the weekends.

I'm jealous.

When my gaze travels back up to his square, shadowed jaw, straight nose, and deep, beautiful eyes, I realize his actions mirror mine. And even standing in the whistling wind with the cold seeping through my bones, I warm in places that have been in hibernation for longer than I care to admit.

His stare bores into me as he takes another step, his

wide chest brushing my arms that are crossed and holding my sweater tight in the cold. His hand comes up—the same hand that I've memorized every single vein—and dips into my hair, gripping the back of my head.

His words are visible in his breath when they hit my face. "Don't tell me to leave."

I want to ask him about his family. About his mother, who he claimed would disown him if he didn't make it back for Christmas. And how he got here in this weather, that no one in their right mind should be out in.

But I don't ask him anything.

All I do is shake my head.

I can't lie, disappointment coursed through my veins when I realized the storm would keep him away. Telling him to leave is the last thing on earth I would do at this moment.

His hold on the back of my head tightens and an energy zips through me—an intensity I knew he had. I could tell from his pictures, the tone of his voice, hell, even his schedule on his phone.

"Haven't thought of anything else but this since you hacked into my phone, Demi."

"I thought you forgave me for that."

"Maybe you should ask for forgiveness for occupying my thoughts. I feel like you've controlled my damn mind. And I don't allow anything or anyone to control me, baby. Ever."

Our breaths visibly dance and swirl in the snowy air. I can't see where one begins and the other ends.

"Tell me you've felt just a little of what I have. Tell me this is an itch you want to scratch," he demands.

"Yes," I answer too fast, because it's more than an

itch. It's irrational and unjustified and completely senseless. Some might go so far as to say foolish. But I don't care. "I'm so happy you're here."

His heated gaze drops to my mouth, his lips follow.

I thought I was warm in remote places before. It's nothing compared to now.

He pulls me to him, our mouths collide, and I'm engulfed in the Italian-American who's a capital P in every sense. And now that he's here in the flesh, I know it to be true. Everything about him is magnificent.

And I'm his itch. He traveled around the world and through a blizzard, missing Christmas with his family. From the sound of it, he'll be disowned by his own mother.

For me.

Our tongues dance, and I shiver when his strong arms circle me. I'm pressed from mouth to thighs with Logan and I'm A-okay with it.

In fact, I'd be okay if it never ended.

My lips meld to his demanding ones. No, they *yield* to his hungry kiss. He tastes like mint and man—I instantly want more of him.

Of anything he'll give me.

I don't know what it is.

The storm bearing down on us.

Feeling small and insignificant in a dangerous winter storm.

The intrigue of meeting a stranger online and getting to know him without actually seeing him in the flesh.

Or it could be everything he is with a capital P.

The Twizzlers and coffee.

Maybe it's the Christmas Spirit.

Whatever it is, it's strong. I realize I'm gripping his

thick corduroy shirt and force myself to pull away from his lips.

I squint up at him through the blizzard swallowing us. "Come inside."

He doesn't answer at first. He leans down and presses his lips to mine once more before pulling in a big breath and making me weak in the knees with his perfect, white smile. "I thought you'd never ask, hacker. It's fucking cold."

TEN
FUCK THE NUMBERS

Logan

Numbers.

There's nothing more trustworthy in the world than numbers. They're the basis of science, our economy, international trade, and even worth.

They also measure the weather. Inches, feet, percentages...

I trust numbers and make informed, intellectual decisions based on them daily. I wipe emotion from the picture. Decisions based on anything other than numbers are for pussies.

Or politicians.

I'm not either.

Or, at least I wasn't last week.

I don't even want to think about what it means that I changed my flight at the last minute to get as close as I could to Winter Falls and Demi, pissed off my mother, and drove a compact-sized rental through the worst blizzard in decades. I've experienced a couple of nor'easters since I moved to the Big Apple, but they've got nothing on this weather phenomenon.

Which supports my theory that trusting the numbers is the way to go one hundred percent of the time.

See there? More numbers.

Even so, right now, I don't give a shit. And since I'm not a pussy and I'm definitely no politician, I've decided I'm nothing other than fucking brilliant. Because, unless she kicks me out into the storm, I'm snowed in with my own personal hacker until further notice. And since she kissed me back when I couldn't wait another second to touch her in the flesh, things are looking good.

Fuck the numbers.

I'm sitting on Demi's sofa and she's obsessing over the cut on my forehead. "What in the hell were you thinking? You could've been killed. No one should be out in this storm, let alone without four-wheel drive."

She's not wrong. Wrapping that Flintstones car around her big-ass pine tree wasn't fun, but it seems everyone else was hell-bent on getting out of Winter Falls when I wanted in, and there was no other rental available. There was barely enough room in the back seat for my backpack.

She's berating me. It's a far cry from her melting in my arms just moments ago in the snow. The space is only lit by a roaring fire and candles, but it's clean, efficient, and I like it. A small tree stands dark in the corner with a cluster of presents tucked beneath.

I feel like I stepped back in time by three decades. I looked up the tax records for her address, for the simple fact I'm nothing if not thorough in everything I do, and it made me feel better since she pretty much read everything on my phone like a best-selling novel. I also know she's a member of the *Winter Falls Snowboarding Club* and the original organizer of *We Climb*.

After I joined the rest of the world on social media, I left my notifications on. If Demi were to try to get hold of me, I wasn't going to miss it, especially since we were on opposite sides of the globe.

What was missing on her social media profiles were men, besides Sheriff Benjamin and her brothers. She's close with her family, which makes me hope if this works out past the weather catastrophe we're experiencing, she might be able to put up with the pain-in-the-ass Carpinos.

She pushes the thick shirt I was using as a coat down my shoulders. It was the heaviest thing I had with me in Australia. I'm thanking the gods it's soaking wet from the snow, because being undressed by my hacker is a bonus I was not counting on.

"It was the only car they had."

She looks up at me, and her eyes are bluer than her pictures let on, even in the dim space. "Are you crazy or stupid?"

I shake my head. "Trust me, I don't normally do shit like this."

"Like what, risk your life?" She shakes the snow from my shirt, drapes it over a chair by the fire, and yanks her sweater down her shoulders.

I probably just missed my first opportunity to undress her too.

Fuck. I don't even recognize myself.

Focus, Logan.

"I only take measured risks. But it seems when a blizzard is going to fuck up my plans, I do things like change my flights and drive hours through the snow." I yank off my shoes since my feet are soaking wet before peeling off my socks. "Trust me, I don't like it either."

Standing there in only leggings and a thin tank top, she crosses her arms over her perfect tits when she shivers. "You should have called me."

I toss my socks on the hearth in front of the fire and turn fully to her. "I had no time. I barely got on another flight. And by the time I finally found a rental, it was too late. I was all in and didn't give a shit what you thought."

Her jaw tightens.

The need to touch her again is strong. I take a step forward and she pulls in a breath when I frame her hips with my hands. "The thought of having to go another week or, hell, even a month since I have to be back in Sydney in January, created a pit in my gut."

With these words, her eyes flare.

"Right." I give her a squeeze and pull her body to mine, lowering my tone. "Demi, I've never felt that before. I owed it to myself to figure out what it meant. I owed it to you. We can put that behind us, I'm here now."

"You're here," she echoes.

"Are you pissed? Please don't tell me you're going to send another company-wide email. I can't go through that twice. I'm already the laughing stock of the company."

She pulls her lips between her teeth, and her blue eyes cringe. "That was the result of rage and frustration. I'm sorry about that."

"Do you rage often?"

Her gaze shifts to the side. "Only when someone tells me something isn't possible."

She hasn't moved from my touch, so I slide a hand up to the middle of her back and smile. "I learned my lesson. I will never underestimate you again."

She unfolds her arms from between us. Her fingers, which she normally uses to dig deep into sensitive and private information, feel their way up my chest over my thermal. "I've never been a pit in anyone's stomach before."

"That you know of," I point out, thinking of the last asshole she met online who's been harassing her. But I keep that to myself, because who wants to talk about a stalker at Christmas?

A small smile plays on her lips. "True. I think I have some butterfly bandages for your cut. Are you hungry? I'm afraid we won't have power for a while. I wasn't planning on company for a few days. We'll have to make do."

I can't lie. My mom was pissed when I told her I wouldn't make it to Omaha for Christmas. I explained something came up and I had to change my plans. After that, I turned my phone off because notifications are from the devil himself.

"I'm starving. And my suitcase went to Nebraska. I have a toothbrush in my backpack, but that's it."

Demi grins. "Sounds like a dystopian Christmas special."

I fight the corner of my lips tugging toward the North Pole and exhale. This is going to be interesting.

And I can't fucking wait.

ELEVEN

VULNERABLE

Demi

My contribution to Christmas dinner was supposed to be Brussels sprouts and a buffalo chicken appetizer. I had the appetizer mixed up and ready to bake, but that's it. The temp in my house is falling as fast as the snow outside. Cold dip didn't sound good.

Logan whipped up a rack in the fireplace from a baking sheet. It took longer than normal and it wasn't baked evenly, but we ate warm dip for dinner and had toasted brown sugar glazed Pop Tarts for dessert. If I had to guess, I'd bet Logan Carpino is still hungry, but he hasn't complained.

Now we're sitting in front of the fire, me criss cross, and Logan is leaning back on one arm with his long legs stretched out next to me. We're on our second round of beers and the crackle of the fire is loud, in comparison to the silent night with everything powered off.

I try to bite back the goofy grin on my face, but fail.

He takes a swig of his beer and frowns. "What?"

I let out a little laugh. "I have to admit, from the moment you weren't being an asshole, I wondered what you were like. Never in my wildest imagination did I picture you sitting in my house wearing my Victoria's Secret hoodie and fuzzy socks."

Logan, confident and masculine, is comfortable in his skin. He has to be. He didn't even flinch when I offered him something warm to wear. Size wise, I'm a small, sometimes a medium. But Victoria's Secret sent me the wrong size last year and I forgot to return it. Plus, it's big and roomy—I like to snuggle up in it.

But it is pink with the logo in glitter on the front. And the fuzzy socks he borrowed are red and white striped, a gift from Posey in a Christmas basket that included a vibrator, because she's the best kind of friend.

He nudges my ass with his candy-caned foot and dazzles me with a smile that would make Santa jealous. "I'm a lot of things, hacker, but I've never been prepared for surprise detours or blizzards."

My smile turns tight, and I have to fake my cheery tone. It's stupid, I know. I have no hold on Logan. Just because he flew the opposite direction than his first destination and risked death in a blizzard, he's only been here for a short time. I have no claim on him. "So you plan on doing this again?"

"Fuck, no." He sets his beer down on the floor next to him. "Next time I'll tell you. Maybe you can pick me up a pair of sweats and some boxers for the occasion."

I look down at the bits of paper I'm collecting from

picking the label off my beer because I don't sit idly well.

"Demi."

I look up at his shadowed face lit only by the fire. "Hmm?"

He doesn't move, but that doesn't mean his eyes don't spear me to my spot here on the floor. "Never thought I'd travel around the world and schlep through a blizzard for anyone, let alone someone I met online and who embarrassed me at my place of business. Why are you making that face? Do you want me to leave?"

"No," I exclaim, not cool or smooth or collected.

I have zero play and I know it. I've always been this way. Maybe it's from growing up with brothers. Maybe it's because I'd rather be on a black diamond or hiking the hard trails. Who am I kidding? I'm sure it's because I work behind a keyboard and don't interact with people on a daily basis.

"I don't want you to go. You traveling all the way here to meet me is…" My tongue sneaks out to wet my dry lips. "Well, if this isn't common for you, then *I* really don't do this." I motion back and forth between us. "Why do you think I was on a dating app to begin with? And the only experience I had other than you was not a good one."

"About your bad experience." Logan scoots closer to me and moves my beer out of the way. His hand finds mine and our fingers lace so naturally, it calms my nerves and revs my anxious heart. I wonder if this is how lovers feel when magnetism and instinct take over. If this is what home feels like? "How did that end? I talked to your dad that night, but beyond that, I don't know anything."

His thumb swipes my wrist—back and forth and back and forth. I sense it's to calm me, but it's doing the opposite.

"My dad wants me to file a restraining order. I don't know. I'll see after the holidays."

He gives my hand a squeeze and lets go, moving back to where he was. "My barging in on you. Probably not a good move right now, huh?"

I shake my head and close the space he just created. "Call it intuition, or maybe it's simply the fact I've combed through your phone. I'm glad you're here, Logan. The fact that Sam is an asshole doesn't make you one."

He claims my hand as his again, but this time his hold is tighter. Coupled with his dark gaze, a shiver runs down my spine.

His tone is as low and as warm as the fire light surrounding us. "I'm relieved."

The vibes I get from Logan couldn't be more different than those from Sam.

"You cold?"

If he only knew. Still, I answer, "Yes."

"Come here." He gives me a gentle yank and pulls me between his legs. I turn and fit myself to him. His chest is warm against my back, firm and inviting, as he wraps his arms around me. "Relax, Demi. Been a long couple of days. I traveled over twenty-four hours, drove through a blizzard, and wrapped my rental around a tree. I'm beat."

I lean my head against his shoulder and realize how tired I am too. Not that I've spent an entire day traveling back in time, but between work, getting ready for Christmas, and now my surprise visitor, exhaustion has set in.

His lips brush my ear. "Tell me something about you. Something that will make me feel closer to you. Anything."

Well. My exhaustion just flew out my drafty windows.

The fire does funny things to my eyes as I stare into the flames. Logan says nothing more, letting his probing question hang between us in the silent night. He does run his big hand up and down my arms, the friction warming me.

"You make me nervous," I whisper, and his hands stop, so I keep talking. "In a good way. The best way." His methodical hands move again, and I feel him exhale. "I like it, but I'm scared of it."

He hikes a leg and reclines back against my sofa, taking me with him. "Why are you scared of it?"

I allow myself to settle into his chest. "Because I feel vulnerable. And now that I just admitted this … exposed."

His arms convulse around me, but he says nothing.

My eyes slide to the right. "Isn't this the time you reciprocate with a deep, dark secret not found on your cell?"

His chest vibrates when he presses his lips to the top of my head. "Sorry, I was thinking."

"What about?"

"Being vulnerable is good. We're in our most basic state when we're vulnerable, right? Not sure there's a better time for that than now. Snowed in, no electricity, no distractions."

"That's not a secret, Logan."

"It's been a long time since I've been with a woman. In any way, baby."

I look down at his arms wrapped around me and

trace a vein in his hand with my index finger. "You mentioned that. How long?"

He brings that hand to my chin, tilting my face to his. He presses his lips to mine again, and just like when we were outside in the snow, his kiss is warm, strong, and demanding. His tongue invades my mouth, and I was right before. He's hungry, but not for food.

When he finally allows me to take a breath, he murmurs against my lips. "*Years* long. So, a long fucking time."

I smile.

His eyes narrow.

"You like that?" he asks.

I try to bite back my smile, but it's futile. "Maybe."

He pulls in a breath and turns me back to the fire, in a way I wonder if he's controlling himself. Holding himself back. He mutters, "Talk about exposed."

I settle into him and feel much better about my vulnerable state. When I close my eyes, Logan presses his lips to my temple. "Tomorrow, my beautiful hacker, we'll get to know each other more. Close your eyes."

I do. With the wind and snow lashing against my house, and the nerves swirling in my stomach, I force myself to close my eyes. And I finally relax in the arms of the man who pissed me off so much, I hacked into his phone.

Craziest Christmas ever.

And, maybe, the best.

TWELVE
MY FIRE NEEDS WOOD

Demi

My back is on fire, but the tip of my nose is frozen.

Not literally. But I've never been so hot and cold at the same time.

When I open my eyes, my family room is bathed in light. Snow is still falling in buckets so thick, I can barely see the forest. Beyond that, the mountain range is nowhere to be seen. It's a whiteout.

The fire is barely crackling, but the last thing I want to do is get up and throw another log on the fire. And that's because the man I accidentally met on a dating app and subsequently hacked is wrapped around me.

Logan's thick thigh is hitched and heavy on my hip and legs. His even breaths whisper against my temple. And his hand…

His hand somehow made its way up my shirt, resting warm against my heart and over my breast. I not only feel it, but my hand is holding it there with our fingers woven and warm and so very, very together.

I give his hand a squeeze, and his body contracts around mine. Every muscle is hard and taut as we're wrapped around one another under my down comforter.

One very important part of his body is hot, hard, and pressed into my bottom.

And I like it.

My eyelids fall shut, and I can't help but arch.

His hand that's teasing the swell of my breast inches up, wraps around my neck, and slides to my jaw. He lifts my face as his lips touch the skin below my ear. A shiver runs through my body that has nothing to do with the electricity outage or the frozen state of my nose.

After tasting my skin, the cold tip of his nose brushes my earlobe. "Merry Christmas."

I burrow deeper into his warmth, which also means his cock. I swear it's bigger than it was moments ago and I suddenly hope the snow never stops falling. This feeling could easily become an addiction. "Hmm, merry Christmas."

He presses his groin into my ass. "The fire needs wood."

I bite back a moan because I agree. My *fire* definitely needs *wood*. "Yes."

My head hits his shoulder, and the hand that has a firm grip on my jaw slowly makes its way down the center of my body, teasing my breasts on the way. "You cold?"

"No." I open my eyes. His hair is a gorgeous mess, and his dark gaze holds mine hostage—asking me, willing me, or, maybe even daring me—as his fingers tease my lower abs.

I press my ass into his cock again, and his whole body tenses, his hand flattens on my lower abs and holds me to him. That's right before he slides that hand down the front of my joggers and straight into my panties.

His gorgeous face disappears from my sight when my eyelids fall shut, and I'm lost in Logan Carpino. He doesn't take his time or mess around, which is so like everything I've gotten from him so far. His fingers slide easily between my legs, two fingers plunging deep in my sex.

"Yes. Oh, yes." My words slip out on an exhale, spurring him on. I forget about the snow, our lack of electricity, Christmas, and how we got to this moment. I only focus on exactly what he's doing now. I forget about his thick cock on my ass and press my hips forward.

He pumps me twice before giving me what I want. When he brushes my clit the first time, I gasp.

So fucking good.

"You're so fucking wet."

Yes. Yes, I am.

"For me," he goes on. "You're wet for me."

This is a given, but I don't confirm because I can't form words. For him, my body is reacting in ways I don't recognize. And it's been so long since anyone has caught my interest, let alone had this effect on me.

He circles my clit in a way that might drive me mad if he doesn't kick it into gear soon, putting those muscles to work.

"Please," I beg. "I want more."

"I'll give you whatever you want." Another circle,

this time with just enough pressure to jack my body temperature to the next level. "In time, I'll give you everything. But for now, I'll settle for making you come so hard, you'll forget everything in the world but me."

Wrapped up in one another, I do exactly as he says. I forget what day it is. Where I am. That the man who kept me warm all night, who currently has his hand down my pants, works halfway around the world, and when he isn't, he lives in New York City.

I have no idea what will happen after this. I should care. It's in my nature to care.

But I just don't.

I'm going to do something that isn't me. Hooking up with someone I only met last week online might be reckless to some. It normally would be to me.

But the man traveled for more than twenty-four hours. He skipped Christmas with his family. He drove a compact car through a snowstorm. He wrapped that car around a tree.

All to meet me. To see me in the flesh.

I'll offer up my flesh to him on a Cookies for Santa platter at this point.

He rolls me to my back. "Spread."

I let my knees fall to the sides, and he takes my mouth. His hand dips farther between my legs, not teasing any longer. His thumb takes control of my clit, which becomes the motherboard for the rest of my body.

Thoughts dissolve.

Stars explode.

Oxygen evaporates.

I pant, moan, and shake beneath his touch.

He takes my mouth again with such force, my moans feeding his drive. His body covers mine, his cock replacing his hand as he presses into my core, driving me wild despite the layers between us.

Damn the invention of clothes.

He's breathing hard despite the fact he hasn't come. The evidence is still pressed to my sex. "Did that warm you up?"

When I open my eyes with nothing in my view but him, caging me, and looming over me, I admit, "My nose isn't frozen anymore."

"Nothing on you is frozen, hacker. If this is how we're forced to keep each other warm through the blizzard, I'll happily stay forever."

I hitch my leg and pull my foot up over his firm ass to hold him tight, because I want more.

But before I have a chance to say anymore, my cell rings where it's sitting on the coffee table. Logan starts to reach for it, but I stop him. "No, I don't want to talk to anyone."

He ignores me. "Someone is calling you on Christmas during a blizzard. I doubt it's a client. You don't want anyone coming to look for you. Selfishly, I don't want anyone to come looking for you."

He's right. And the last thing I want to explain to anyone is who Logan is or why he's here.

I barely glance at the screen before pressing the button to answer, and I'm glad I did. Logan stays where he is as I greet my father. "Hey, Dad."

"Cell service has been spotty. I've been trying to call you for an hour."

I look up at Logan and smile. "I'm good. Merry Christmas."

"Merry Christmas. Your mom is having a fit with you being there by yourself. You okay?"

Logan's lips hit my neck as I speak. "Yeah, I'm good. No need to worry about me."

"As long as you're staying warm."

Logan makes it hard to even my tone. He palms my breast and runs his lips across my collarbone. "No problem staying warm. Plenty of wood."

With that one word, Logan presses his groin into me again, and I grip his shirt. I'm not sure if I'm holding him to me or pushing him away.

"This is supposed to go on for a while. Could add up to a couple of feet of snow. Keep your fire going. They're working on getting the power up."

I nod—as if he can see me—and keep my answers short and simple. "Okay."

My dad pauses. "You okay?"

"Yeah, no. I mean, yes, I'm fine. Just woke up, that's all." Logan peeks up at me and grins. And if what he was doing to my body wasn't enough, that grin is so uncharacteristic of him, it takes my breath away.

"Okay. When I can get over there, I'll plow your drive."

Cold air hits my skin. I look down and Logan's playful grin is gone. He's pushed my cardigan sweater to the side and pulled my tank down, exposing my breast, as his expression turns hungry, taking in my body.

Warm lips and tongue capture my nipple, and my head hits the throw pillow. I pull in a shaky breath. "No hurry, Dad. I'm fine, really."

For the first time in my life, I'm thankful my father has a job that requires him to work on holidays. "I've got to go. If you can believe, idiots still think they can get out in this weather. People are stuck left and right. It's like they're desperate to get somewhere.

If they're anything like Logan, I get their desperation. "Be careful, Dad."

The moment I toss my phone to the floor, Logan pulls my nipple between his teeth before letting go to move to my face.

"Now you stop?" I complain. "That was torture."

He leans down to kiss me. "The fire needs to be fed. I need to be fed. I've also traveled around the world. As tempting as you are, I'm not fucking you for the first time after two days without a shower."

I let that thought linger as I reach up and trace his lower lip with my thumb.

"If that's where this is going," he amends.

My gaze lifts to his dark eyes as my teeth sink into my lower lip. "Then, I guess that means I need to manually light my old hot water heater. I wouldn't want you to have to take a cold shower."

His eyes flare with intensity before he kisses me and rolls. The cool air assaults me as we twist in the comforter. He brings his knees up, my legs part, and his hands land on my ass with a tight squeeze. "This might just be the best Christmas ever."

A slow smile creeps across my face, because I agree.

THIRTEEN
CHEERS TO GRAY SWEATPANTS

Logan

I flip off the water and grab the towel she put out for me. Losing power must not be a rare occurrence in the mountains, because Demi knew exactly how to light the pilot on her water heater. As much as I wanted to wash her myself, I ignored my feelings and let her shower first.

I'll never travel again without a change of clothes.

She dug through a trunk in her basement and found an old pair of sweats that at least aren't a size small, even though I can tell they're still too small for me. Biting back a smile, she handed me a T-shirt that shows her support to *Free Brittney*. She said she bought it oversized to cover her ass.

I told her there was no reason to ever cover her ass. I'm stealing her shirt for that very reason.

She laughed and lifted onto her toes to press her lips to mine.

Then I picked her up and tossed her to the bed

before covering her body with mine and decided I'm moving her mattress to the family room in front of the fire. After the long plane ride and sleeping on the floor, my back is a pretzel.

As tempting as it was to continue how we started Christmas morning, I needed a shower.

I slip on the wool ski socks that are too small, grab my pink Victoria's Secret sweatshirt, and run my fingers through my wet hair.

Everything about Demi's house is old. But it's at the top of the mountain—I should know since I risked my life getting here. I'm sure when there's not a blizzard, there's a view of the range. But the carpet is worn, the tile is cracked, and I doubt her fixtures look any better when there's electricity running to them.

Cinnamon, vanilla, and coffee fill the house as I make my way out of her bedroom and down the stairs. When I round the corner, she's standing at her old gas stove stirring something in a pot and sipping from a mug.

I lean against the door jamb and cross my arms. "You're lucky I'm comfortable in my masculinity."

She turns and studies me from head to toe. It's not lost on me that her gaze hesitates over my cock before it jumps back to my face. She puts her mug to her lips one more time before licking them. "Hey, I gave you everything but underwear."

"I know."

Her head cocks to the side. "What did you do? Turn your dirty ones inside out?"

"No fucking way. Do you think I'm barbaric?" I hitch a shoulder. "Commando."

Her stare turns into a gape and drops straight back to my cock. And since he has a mind of his own and remembers when I teased him earlier, half the blood in my body rushes straight to him.

"Demi," I call for her.

"Hmm?" She finally looks away from my dick.

I try not to smile. "You okay?"

She lifts her mug and doesn't hide her smirk. "Cheers to gray sweatpants that are too small. Merry Christmas to me."

"Are you objectifying me? I feel like you did this on purpose."

"Would you rather I have men's clothing lying around? You're lucky to have what you have."

"Meanwhile you look like the Pillsbury Doughboy, you've got so many layers on."

Her eyes widen. "It's cold. I'll freeze."

I push off the wall, move to her, and steal her mug. After taking a big gulp, I ask, "Did you make coffee for me too?"

She lifts her chin to the orange countertop that looks about fifty years old. "I have enough coffee for years, and my new French press came in handy. I'll pour you a cup. How do you take it?"

I can't wait another second. I put her coffee down on the counter and rest my hands on either side of her, caging her in. "Black."

"I can see that. People who drink black coffee tend to be intense."

"As opposed to you who drinks a little bit of coffee with her sugary creamer?"

Her smile is sly. "What can I say? I'm not intense. I'm sweet."

I press her into the counter. There's not going to be anything left to the imagination if I don't get a handle on my dick soon. "Baby, you hacked into my company and my cellphone. I would not call you sweet."

She pokes a finger in my chest. "But I told them how to fix it."

"You didn't tell me how to fix my phone. I think you still want to have a peek from time to time."

"You figured me out." She smiles bigger. "I made oatmeal for breakfast. Not very special for Christmas, but it's the best I can do on the stovetop. I'm saving scrambled eggs for lunch. We'll have Twizzlers for dessert."

I run my hands up her sides before lifting her to the counter. She parts her legs for me, and when I step between them, I hardly feel her for all the layers she's wearing. I was not kidding about the Doughboy look she's sporting. With my hands on her layered ass, I pull her to me. "I'm moving your mattress in front of the fire. I don't want you to get too cold when I give you your Christmas present."

"Why would I be any colder than I am now? And you got me a present?"

I lean in and kiss her. "A big present. But you'll be naked."

She fists my Victoria's Secret sweatshirt. "I love Christmas. Please keep me warm."

"I'll always keep you warm, hacker." I dip my hand down the back of her pants and feel her skin-to-skin again. "Now, pour me a cup of coffee."

FOURTEEN
THE FORESTRY COMMISSION

Demi

Gray sweatpants are a gift from the universe. Especially when they're two sizes too small and hug every inch, curve, and bulge.

I didn't even try to hide it. I ogled, oohed, and awed over the display Logan Carpino put on. And after he kissed me crazy on my counter, I got to watch him walk out of my kitchen and could see almost every flex of his glutes—all maximus, medius, and minimus of them. They were beautiful. I thought I was looking forward to my present before, but now I really can't wait. Getting naked with Logan just jumped to the top of my Christmas list.

I've never had a man surprise me during a blizzard before. Actually, no man has ever surprised me with much of anything before.

I was not prepared for Logan Carpino. I mean, a woman does a lot to prepare for a simple night out.

The level of maintenance required for an overnight guest belongs in an entirely different realm.

A different universe.

After this morning, I knew there would be naked fun in my near future, which meant I had work to do.

And goodness knows, it's been a long time since I've spent considerable time on any of that maintenance.

I took a long shower and I didn't apologize for it. I shaved parts that the forestry commission would have deemed unsafe to venture into. My woodlands have been private for so long, there was no need for trimming, thatching, or keeping the underbrush clear.

The forest has been wiped from the face of my planet. There will be no saving the trees in my future. I wiped it clean out of existence. I even pulled a muscle in the process, but I stretched it out.

I'm no quitter. The nooks and crannies of a network aren't the only things I'm good at weaseling my way into.

But I'm ready—as fresh as the snow falling outside. So much so, I'm afraid to open my back door.

Not that back door. My literal back door.

So much snow.

While I made a fresh carafe of coffee and dished up the least fancy Christmas breakfast in the history of candy canes, Logan did what he promised. Like it was no biggie, he pushed all my family room furniture to the side and dragged my queen mattress in front of the fire. By the time we sat down with our oatmeal, he had it roaring.

"What made you get into mergers and acquisitions?"

Just like last night, I'm sitting criss cross, and Logan

is stretched out on his side again, propped on an elbow. We're facing one another, and I'm hitting him rapid fire with questions. With the gray sweatpants situation going on down there, I have to force myself to focus on his face.

Focus, Demi.

His index finger traces the vein inside my wrist. "Got a scholarship for my undergrad, but not my master's. My number one goal was to pay off my student loans, so I took the best compensation package I was offered. Salaries and bonus structures like mine right out of school aren't typical. I knew they expected grueling hours and a majority of time on the road. But I paid off my school loans in two years and now I'm debt free."

"You own your place in Manhattan?"

His lips tip up on one side, and he shakes his head. "If I remember correctly, you complimented my compensation package. Do you really need to ask that?"

I shrug and look around at my house that's lacking in everything but location and view. "I've never lived anywhere but Winter Falls. My house wasn't cheap. I have a mortgage, but most people do."

"I work with companies who get themselves in a shit ton of trouble because they don't know how to manage their money. They're slaves to their debt. I never want to feel that way. My place might be in Manhattan, but it's not huge. Don't get me wrong, it's the shit, and I love it. I don't bother with stuff I don't want and or need cluttering my life."

I look down at our fingers that are now threaded. I push up his pink sleeve and study his forearm. The strong arm, veins, and olive skin that got my attention that first day I opened his profile on Force of Nature and he was flipping me off. I can't look up at him when I add, "Yet, you're here."

"I am."

There's something in his tone, and my gaze travels up. "Why?"

His lips purse before he shakes his head slowly. "I'm trying to figure that out myself."

My insides tighten.

He grabs my hand and holds tight, his warmth traveling through me. "I mean that in the best way possible. Changing my plans at the last minute, driving through a blizzard, and showing up unannounced at a woman's house I've never met in person is not like me. But something inside drove me to do it."

I pull in a breath and try to calm the storm raging within, so wicked, it rivals the one happening outside.

"There was no option. No choice," he adds. "I knew I had to be here with you."

"How did we end up here? We never should've met. You didn't even put your profile up. I didn't swipe on it. And really, after what I did, you should hate me. But instead, you sent me Twizzlers and coffee. This shouldn't be happening, Logan."

He tips his head. "It's fate."

"It's magic." A smile breaks over my face, and my eyes widen. "The Christmas Spirit."

He leans back and pulls me with him. Falling to his chest, he grabs me behind the knees and hikes my legs up his sides. My hair, still damp from the shower, curtains us. "If it was, I'm pissed the Christmas spirit wrapped my rental around a tree and gave me a knot on the head. I was already here—I didn't need a kick in the ass."

I turn his face and lightly press my lips to his temple where the bandage is still in place. "I'm sorry you were hurt."

He captures my chin between his thumb and forefinger turning my mouth to his. His tongue delves in my mouth, and he grips my hair to hold me to him. There's a desperation in his kiss, not at all like we're in the middle of a blizzard, going nowhere fast, and all we have is time.

No, it's like he can't wait another second.

He pulls me back a fraction and he swallows hard. "From the moment I realized you hacked me, I haven't been able to get you out of my mind. First trying to figure you out, then wanting to find you. Then you went from hacker to sweet, and I wanted nothing more than to race across the world to meet you in person. I don't give a shit what brought us here, baby, I'm just glad it did. I can't believe I'm saying this, but my damn brother and brother-in-law putting me in your path, might be the best thing that's ever happened to me. Not that I'll ever admit that to them."

"Serendipity," I whisper.

"Baby." He slides a hand under all three layers of shirts and sweaters I'm wearing. "It was a fluke. I accidentally met a woman who is likely smarter than me, and I took full advantage."

I shake my head as his big hand warms me, sliding up my spine. "Stop it. It was divine, and I refuse for you to make it anything less."

He lifts his hips, but I don't feel him as much as I'd like because of my leggings and joggers. "A lucky fucking break, and now you might just be stuck with me."

"Nope. It's definitely kismet. I refuse to believe otherwise."

Logan leans up to kiss me quickly as his hand travels south, dipping into all the layers I'm sporting. It's ironic that I feel so very unsexy for the man who sets my butterflies free like no one ever has. When his hand travels over the swell of my ass and dips between my legs, he freezes.

My butterflies ditch me in an instant, and I push up to look at him. "What's wrong?"

He grips my sex, and I can't decide if I like it or not, before narrowing his eyes. "This feels very different than it did this morning."

My face warms, and my heart speeds. It has nothing to do with the roaring fire.

His fingers slide through my now bare folds.

Naked, in every sense.

Exposed.

And, again, vulnerable.

Just like my soul at the moment. What was I thinking? I hardly know him. I certainly never thought he'd call me out on it. I thought he might like it and carry on with business.

He is *businessy*, after all.

But, you know, silently.

The next thing I know, I'm on my back, and Logan is kneeling on the mattress at my feet. "I'm not sure how I thought this would go." He yanks one of my fuzzy socks off and reaches for the other one. "Swear to you, hacker, I had no expectations. None." He reaches for my waist, but I'm too dazed by his expression to care. "I was desperate and I'm never desperate. Surprising a woman who is little more than a stranger during a blizzard at Christmas was not my best move. I felt lucky you didn't make me sleep in a snowbank after I crashed into your tree. I was just happy you didn't hate me." My joggers land with my socks, and he reaches for my leggings. "Good God, how do women wear these? They're practically painted on."

I lift my hips, and he puts some muscle into dragging them over my ass. "They're compression. They're supposed to be tight."

"My sweats are tight enough. These must be hell," he mutters, wrestling one leg at a time over my feet. My leggings are in knots when he's done, and goosebumps run up my body from my toes to my panties. He sits back on his calves and pulls in a big breath, as if undressing my layers were a workout. Then, his gaze travels slowly up my body, him following, prowling over me like some wild animal who just pantsed his prey and intends to enjoy his Christmas feast.

"Logan—"

"Shh." He leans on a forearm as I take his weight. This time, I feel every delicious inch of his commando cock pressing between my legs. Only my panties and his too-small joggers keep us from one another. My clit daydreams about the way we woke up this morning. He presses his lips to mine, and I drag a bare leg over his rock-hard ass. He lifts his head an inch and exhales. "I study data for a living. The fact your pussy is now bare is telling me you might want more."

My teeth find my lip.

"If I were to make a projection, I'd say you want everything," he goes on.

"You really like analyzing data, huh?"

He presses his cock into my needy clit again. "I'd like to analyze all your data. I might become obsessed with it."

I draw my leg up farther, bringing my knee up to his side. "I might've … done a little housekeeping. You know, just in case."

His stare lingers before his tone lowers. "Serendipity."

A small smile forms on my lips. "I told you so."

He kisses me and then mutters there, "If it weren't fifty degrees in here, I'd strip you bare. We'll save that for when the electricity comes on. I'll do my best to keep you warm."

I lose his weight and his warmth, his fingers hooking my panties at the hips. Slowly, he peels them down my legs and never looks away from my body as my panties flutter over his shoulder and land across the room. He pushes my knees apart. My head falls back, and I close my eyes. My body jerks when his touch comes light on the inside of my thigh and trails to ground zero.

"I like your kind of housekeeping," he mutters, and I hear him move.

When I open my eyes, I see nothing but a full head of dark wavy hair descending between my legs.

"Holy shit," I mutter.

"Yes." His tongue trails my pubic bone and he agrees, "Holy shit. I think I like blizzards, and I could spend Christmas right here for the rest of my life."

I gasp, but can't add any commentary or freak out. Because this turns into National Geographic all over again. Logan is the lion, and I am very much his prey.

And my lion is hungry.

His hands grip my ass, and he lifts. Holding me to his mouth. Devouring me.

I thought this morning was good, but now I think he was teasing me, barely giving me a taste of his skills.

Moans bleed from my lips. I'm not cold anymore. My body is humming and I have to grip the blanket below me to hang on. Not that I can control anything. I'm completely under Logan's spell.

And I'm not sure I want that to change.

I slap the mattress, but it's weak. "Oh … oh … oh, please. Don't stop."

Logan doesn't stop.

His fingers bite into the delicate skin on my hips. His tongue teases me from sex to clit and back again.

But when he smothers my clit with his lips and sucks, I fall.

Moaning, my hearing tunnels, and I see nothing but fireworks.

I lose his mouth but gain his weight. Logan's lips hit mine and he kisses me with more energy than a pack of Santa's elves on a deadline.

"Baby," he murmurs against my lips. "I don't have a condom, but I'm clean."

I open my eyes and reach down, palming his long, hard cock, begging to be set free from my new favorite pants. "Then it's good I'm on birth control. I'm clean too. Please, I want all of you."

"You're sure?" He hesitates. "If you want to wait, I get it—"

I lift my head to shut him up with my lips and squeeze him as best I can through the thin material

He takes over my kiss and reaches down to push his pants out of the way.

And finally.

My asshole from a dating app, who turned out to be a dream, makes me his.

He pushes in. He might've been sweet just moments ago, but there's nothing sweet or gentle about him now. Want and need take over, his desperation seeps into me when he slams inside. Every gorgeous inch of him stretches me.

It's official—Logan Carpino feels good everywhere.

He groans and stays planted deep. "Fuck, Demi."

"I know, right?" I hitch my legs up his sides, and he slips an arm under the small of my back. I didn't think it possible, but he slides in even farther, touching places inside me I didn't know existed.

He starts to move, and it's even better. It's all Logan, and I'm here for it. I might take everything he's willing to give. If that's desperate and needy, I don't care.

He pumps into me harder and faster. Besides the crackling fire, the only sounds to be heard are our breaths and bodies becoming one.

He touches that place deep inside me, and my body constricts. Logan's muscles tense. His cock connects two more times, and I come again, harder and more intense than ever before.

I'm pressed into the mattress with Logan—spent and breathing hard—on top of me. I run my fingers through his hair and he turns his face to me, pressing his lips to my temple like he's done so many times.

Or as many times as someone can in the matter of twenty-four hours.

He doesn't move other than reaching for the comforter lying on the floor and throwing it over us. "Keep you warm."

I take in his deep brown eyes and messy hair. "If this is how you keep me warm, don't ever stop."

His lips spread into a devastating smile.

I know the snow will fade eventually.

The power will buzz again.

And real life will commence.

I have no idea what that will bring.

For now, all I want is to ignore reality. This is turning out to be the best Christmas ever.

FIFTEEN
SCORE ONE FOR MATH NERDS

Logan

When you become an adult, Christmas is Christmas. It's a day your mother bosses you around, you overeat, over drink, and go through the motions of your big-ass Italian family, because should you miss, you'll eat shit until the Fourth of July.

Been there, done that. Not worth the drama in the Carpino family.

But as a kid, Christmas was the best day of the year, aside from my birthday.

When I was seven, I asked for my first set of golf clubs. I wrote letters to Santa, begged my parents, and even sweet-talked my grandpop. There was nothing I wanted more.

I got my wish that year, and my parents went all out. They even came with head covers of my favorite superheroes. I couldn't use them until the snow melted, but I slept with my putter every night until spring.

Nothing beat my first set of clubs. I still have them at my parents' house. That was the best Christmas ever.

Until today.

And I wonder if this is just a little taste of why everyone else in my family still goes apeshit over a holiday I force myself to squeeze into my schedule.

Christmas dinner consists of tacos, macaroni and cheese, and craft beer from the local brewery. For dessert, it's apple slices with peanut butter and Twizzlers. I didn't realize when I ordered the Twizzlers just how many it would be. I got her attention, and that's all that matters.

And right now, the only way I'm going anywhere is if I take my hacker with me.

I've learned a lot about Demi Benjamin on my favorite Christmas ever. She likes good beer, easy food, and by the menu, she was not at all prepared for a blizzard. But she has enough firewood for the next ten years, so we should be good.

We eat. We talk. We drink.

Her eyes come alive when she explains how she breaks into networks. How she loves each new challenge, likes working for herself, and does her best work at night so she can snowboard or hike during the day. She explains how she was an awkward teenager who'd rather play video games with her brothers than shop or experiment with makeup.

For some reason, sitting in the middle of a blizzard, commando in too-small pants with a Victoria's Secret sweatshirt, apparently peels the layers off a man. I'm not a sharer by nature, but for some reason nothing felt more basic than telling Demi that I was the skinny, awkward, math whiz until my senior year. Despite my height, I didn't make the basketball team in high school because the coach said I'd get snapped in two.

Since I wasn't popular and didn't play sports, I pretty much dominated the Quiz Bowl Team, was president of the math club, and lettered in debate my freshman year.

It wasn't until college that I put on some muscle, but when you spend that much time devoted to brainiac activities and not attending parties because you weren't invited, there's pretty much no going back.

I might've come into my own late and can splurge on custom-made suits, but I was, and will always be, a math nerd. My older brother, Grant, still gives me shit for it. My younger sister, Avery, loves me for it. It might be because I did her homework for her, but I know she'd love me anyway.

So, I gave a piece of me to Demi for Christmas since her actual gift is in my suitcase, hopefully in Omaha by now.

When I got to the part of my story that included me getting hazed as a sophomore because I refused to let Scott Duvall, a senior and the star quarterback, copy my trigonometry homework, Demi closed the two feet separating us on the mattress, wound her legs around my waist, and shut me up with her lips.

She ripped off my pink sweatshirt.

Then she gave me the best Christmas present ever. She stood, stripped down to nothing, and returned to my lap. A shiver moved through her body when she fit herself to my bare chest. "I've never wanted anyone more, Logan."

Score one for math nerds everywhere. Maybe I

should be pissed I haven't capitalized on that shit sooner, but I just don't care. I'm glad I saved my internal nerd for Demi.

Her breaths are hot at my temple, her arms wrapped around my neck, and her grip on my hair is pulling at the roots. If I die from lack of oxygen because she's holding on too tight while she rides my hand, it will suck because this only lasted a day.

"You can do it, baby. Make yourself come."

I turn my head when she throws her head back, her long, dark hair falling down her bare back. I put my lips to her collar bone and suck. She groans, causing me to suck harder. The thought of marking her makes my dick swell even more.

I lift my head to look at the beauty in my lap. "You want it, you're going to have to move, hacker."

She's close. I feel it and see it and hear it. So fucking wet, but I'm not helping. This is all her. I'm here for the show.

With her feet dug into the mattress behind me, she rocks forward.

"Good girl." I encourage her. "Do it again."

She gives me her blues, and they've never been so sexy, hooded and seeping lust. For me.

"Do it again, Demi," I command.

She leans back, and her small tits bounce when she moves to rub against my fingers. I'm cupping her as lightly as I can. I want to watch her work for this. "Please, Logan."

I shake my head and lean in to kiss her. "This is all you. Do this for me."

She tips her forehead to mine. Our lips brush, our noses side-by-side. I've now had my hands and lips on every inch of her—and it's not enough.

I've never wanted to be closer to anyone. To never want it to end. It doesn't matter that my dick is about to explode, and I have no other clean clothes to my name, she could do this until next Christmas, and it wouldn't last long enough.

She wants it, because she moves, rocking her hips, her body warm from the inside out, and her hair a wild, beautiful mess. I hear and feel her desperation through her pants hot on my skin.

She moves faster and moans. More blood rushes to my dick. Watching her is pure joy and utter torture.

I lose her blue eyes when her head falls back, her jaw goes slack, and she presses hard on my hand. Her moans are sweet music to my ears, so I put my free hand to the middle of her back and wrap my lips around a nipple.

Her grip on my hair tightens, and I bite down on her sensitive skin. She gasps, and I take over, giving her clit more pressure, milking her orgasm for everything it's worth.

But I can't wait any longer. I wrap my arms around her and climb to my knees. Her back barely hits the mattress when I flip her over. I reach down and squeeze one globe of her beautiful ass while yanking my joggers out of the way with the other.

Demi peeks over her shoulder, her gaze goes directly to my cock.

And fuck me, she licks her lips.

"Trust me, hacker, I'm looking forward to fucking your mouth—we'll get to that later. Right now, I want your ass in the air."

I lift her hips and nudge her knees apart. The snow has started to slow enough to see the mountain range, but nothing beats the view of my cock disappearing, inch by inch, in Demi's tight pussy with her beautiful ass on display.

"Yes," she purrs. "So deep."

I silently agree.

Gripping her ass, I don't take it slow. I couldn't if I wanted to. This is different. Our energy is different. This is about scratching the itch we've both felt from the beginning. At least I hope it is for her, because it sure as shit is for me.

"Fuck." I groan and slam into her harder.

My balls draw up. My muscles tense. There's something about her that makes me feel helpless yet more in control than I've ever been, all at the same time.

It makes me want to bang on my chest and jump in a snowbank like a lumberjack on speed.

And if I'm being completely honest, this whole situation makes me question my own judgment. But, I'm pretty fucking happy, so I'm going with it.

When her pussy clenches my dick and holds tight, I lose it. I crash into her two more times before sinking deep and staying there. Demi's cheek is pressed to the mattress, and she's breathing as hard as I am. Catching my breath, I fall forward on my hands and push her flat, covering her, but I don't pull out.

I brush the hair from her face, and murmur, "Best Christmas, baby."

Her eyes come to mine, but her smile is small. "Yeah. It is."

"I'll get the fire going. You get dressed and stay warm."

She nods and looks out the window where the sun is setting. It isn't the whiteout it was earlier.

"Hey," I call.

She looks back to me.

"I'll figure this out." My stare is intense for a reason. It's not lost on me the storm is coming to an end. The holiday will be over, the electricity will return, and life will begin again. "It might not be easy, but I'll do it. Okay?"

She reaches up and traces my jaw with her thumb. If a touch could be contemplative, this would be it.

"Get dressed, baby. I don't want you to get cold."

I kiss her nose and push to stand. Reality is about to smack us in the face, and I'm not looking forward to it.

Shit.

SIXTEEN

CHICKEN

Demi

L ogan really knows his morning brew. I'll never go back to my basic coffee maker. I'm thanking my lucky stars my old, rickety gas stove still works, which means I can at least boil water. This French press is the best thing that's happened to me in years.

Well, the best thing besides my Force of Nature and an accidental meet, which started out like a trip to hell, but turned out to be everything.

A thick arm wraps around my waist, and my back is warmed by solid, hot muscle.

So much more.

"You have an amazing view."

I take a sip of coffee before leaning my head on his shoulder. The fire crackles away at our side as we stand in front of my drafty window. "I know. My house might be falling apart at the seams, but that makes up for it."

Another Christmas has come and gone.

My entire life, we've done the same thing at Christmas. Don't most people? If traditions don't live strong this time of year, when do they?

I never realized traditions make everything blend into one memory. Sure, holiday rituals are nice, warm, and fuzzy. They're comfortable like the ratty pajama pants you just can't get rid of because they feel better with time.

It wasn't until this Christmas that I realized *comfortable* isn't always best. Every detail of this Christmas will be burned on my brain forever. The year I was pushed out of my comfort zone by an accidental meeting with a man who is anything but a stranger now, and a blizzard for the record books.

But the blizzard's coming to an end, just like my days with Logan.

The sun is shining, and Winter Falls is coming back to life again. My mom called this morning, and plows are hitting their streets in town. Their electricity is up and running.

This should make me happy.

"My mother is throwing a fit about Christmas."

I set my coffee down, turn away from the breathtaking view of sun glistening on the snow-covered peaks, and look up at the man who kept me warm for days, in so many ways. "I'm sorry."

He brushes a stray chunk of hair from my face that's too short for my ponytail. "I'm not."

"But you have to be back at work, right?" My insides tense. "In Australia?"

He winds my pony around his hand and tips my head back, his dark gaze intense. "I do. And I can't push that back. I'm close to wrapping up my portion of the acquisition. The next month is critical."

"I feel bad you came all this way, and you won't be able to see your family." That's a lie ... sort of. I do feel bad, but not that bad. I wouldn't change the last few days for anything, not even for his bossy mom.

"I don't. This was the best decision I've ever made." He concurs with my private thoughts and lowers his forehead to mine, our noses brushing. "I make a shit ton of important decisions in my life, but this was by far my best."

"I can't believe it's about over." I push up on my toes and press my body to his. Even though my intent is to kiss him, he takes over and claims my mouth first.

His arms round me and the next thing I know, I'm pressed to the wall. Just when I expect Logan to rip my clothes off and give me another reason to dread his impending departure, he rips his lips from mine and frames my face with his big hands. "Come with me."

My eyes widen, and my breath catches.

He doesn't give me time to speak, agree, or argue. "It's a month. It'll fly by. Call it a vacation. A paid vacation. What difference does it make where you are? The mountains, the beach ... fuck, *Manhattan*," he stresses. I thought my breath caught before, but I might actually pass out from lack of oxygen. "Call it a second date. Hell, call it a trial. I don't give a shit what you call it, but I'm not willing for this to end. If you end up hating me, I'll buy you a first-class ticket back to your mountain. Come with me, Demi. Be with me. Give me a chance. Give *us* a chance."

You'd think I just hiked for hours, that's how difficult it feels to pull in a breath. "I ... I don't know."

"Say yes," he demands. "Say yes, and I'll take care of everything."

Just when I'm about to open my mouth again, the world around us comes to life. Lights flicker. A commercial blares from the TV. The rattling hum of my old furnace begins to chug.

Logan doesn't move.

"Demi—"

I grip his wrists to pull his hands away from my face. Then I make the most lame excuse possible when the perfect man asks me to spend a month with him in Australia. "I need to reset my clocks."

His eyes narrow. "Are you shitting me?"

I shake my head and give his wide chest a push. "They'll blink and drive me crazy. I need to make sure my hot water heater is reset. We can shower and do laundry. Then I need to call my snow removal service and make sure I'm on the list for today. I need to go to the grocery store."

"You're shitting me." This time it's a statement, and not a surprised one.

He's angry. Pissed.

At me.

"You can, um…" I look around and realize there's nothing for him to do. "Never mind. I've got to check the water heater."

"Demi." His growl is guttural and angry. A sound I've never heard pass his lips, not even when he crashed into my tree.

And like the chicken I turn into when unease settles deep within me, I run. Though, I can only escape to the basement since there's still three feet of snow outside.

SEVENTEEN
GO WITH YOUR GUT

Logan

"Sorry, Dad. My plans changed at the last minute, and I got stuck in a blizzard. I have to be back in Sydney after the new year. My project there should wrap at the end of January. I already booked time on my schedule after that to come home."

"Your mom's pissed. Really she's hurt, but she's masking it as pissed."

The power has only been up for an hour. My clothes are already in the dryer and Demi busied herself with every-fucking-thing before she got in the shower. The lane to her house was just plowed, a service shoveled her drive and walk, and a tow truck is loading up my rental.

Winter Falls doesn't mess around when it comes to getting back to business after a storm.

"I'll make it up to her," I promise, but wonder how exactly I'm going to do that. Besides going back in time and missing out on the last few days with Demi—

which I wouldn't trade for anything—there's nothing that will make up missing a Carpino Christmas in my mom's eyes.

"The least you could do is tell us what was so important you changed your plans at the last minute."

What the hell? It's like I'm in high school and didn't show up for dinner. I sigh and drag a hand down my face. "I met someone. I had plans to come here after Christmas, but she was ground zero for a blizzard that moved through. I took a chance and came here first."

The line goes silent.

"Dad?"

"You met someone? You mean, you actually took time out of your schedule—hell, your life—for another human?"

I knew this would happen. Which is why I've been radio silent with every Carpino on earth other than saying I wouldn't make it for Christmas. "This is why I didn't tell anyone."

"Who is it?" he asks.

"A woman. She lives in Winter Falls."

"How did you meet a woman in Winter Falls?"

The tow truck driver finishes and gives me a thumbs up from the snowbank he's trudging through. I'm about to answer, but my damn brother appears in the background. "Logan met a woman?"

Shit.

My father is intent on torturing me. "Let me put you on Facetime."

"Why is my meeting a woman so shocking? I date." The Facetime request comes in, and I sigh before accepting. My fucking family. I hold my phone up and look at the screen. "Hey."

My dad greets me. "Merry Christmas, son."

"Merry Christmas."

"Dude." Grant forces his way in the screen, and is resorting to *dude*. "What the fuck are you wearing? Did you become someone's bitch over Christmas?"

I look down at my pink, bedazzled sweatshirt from a lingerie store and shrug. "I lost my suitcase."

"Link!" Grant yells. "Logan met a woman, and he's wearing shit from Victoria's Secret!"

My dad keeps talking. "What's most shocking—aside from your choice of attire—is that you met a woman you're willing to wander into a blizzard for. I know you and I don't think there's ever been anyone you've been willing to cross the street for. So, yeah. Shocking. I can't wait to tell your mom. She'll drop the pissed and get off my ass about you. But I'll leave out the part about your outfit."

"Dad—" I try but get interrupted.

Grant keeps going. "Tell me you met her online. Make all my dreams come true and tell me I'm the one responsible for you actually finding the one. Was it the one who swiped you?"

"I'm not telling you shit."

Link enters the fray. Good Lord, the Carpinos are always together, even the in-laws. "What the hell are you wearing?"

"A chick swiped on Logan's dating profile we made," Grant explains.

Link is as surprised as the rest of them. "No shit? Who would swipe on that?"

Grant and Link continue an entire conversation without me or Dad. "Right? We're geniuses. Women might say they don't like assholes, but I think they do."

147

"Hey," I butt in. "I'm not an asshole. I'm busy and have a life."

Grant points at me through the screen. "You made Mom cry on Christmas. If you're not an asshole, then I'm not a Carpino. That's beyond the point. Is this the same chick you told me about last week or did our epic profile crash the servers on the dating site?"

I'm about to threaten Grant's ability to have more children, but something else demands my attention.

And that something would be a police cruiser making its way up Demi's lane. It stops and the driver rolls down his window to talk to the tow truck driver, who points to my rental, and the tree.

"Shit," I mutter.

"Did you piss off your new woman already? Don't mess this up. This could be a once-in-a-lifetime shot, and Mom wants more grandkids. You can't leave that shit to Avery and me alone."

As if on cue, my sister appears. "Leave what up to us?"

Link puts an arm around his wife. "Logan met someone online. We're trying to coach him on how not to fuck it up. I think she likes assholes."

"You two are trying to coach Logan?" Avery laughs and looks back at me. "And why go through the process of being an asshole just to have to kiss her ass? Kiss her ass from the beginning. Trust me."

"That's true." Link pulls her in to kiss the top of her head. "You know I enjoy kissing your ass, baby."

Avery slaps his chest. "Stop."

"I've got to go." I don't need to run numbers or use my reasoning skills to tell me this is Demi's dad trudging to the door through the snow. And since I'm still in her clothes, and she's in the shower, this might be awkward.

"Don't listen to them, Logan." I look back at Avery. "Go with your gut. If you want her, do everything you can to make her yours. You don't make it easy on yourself by traipsing all over the world for work."

Don't I know it. And if Demi running away from me when I asked her to come with me is any indication, Avery is right.

Grant disagrees. "I say he stays true to himself. Let your assholeness shine, bro. If she swiped, she's into it."

My dad interjects his last words of wisdom. "Don't listen to your brother. He talks big but he'd be sleeping in the garage if he followed his own advice. Good luck! And call your mom."

"No!" Avery reaches for the phone and I only see her face. "Call me. I need to know everything."

My family. They're fucking crazy. I don't say goodbye but disconnect as Sheriff Benjamin keeps his eyes trained on me.

It might've stopped snowing, but it's still freezing. I don't make him wait and open the door before he makes it up the steps. He crosses the threshold and stomps the snow from his boots.

The main lawman in the county looks me up and down. For the first time in days, I regret going commando. "Seeing as my daughter owns this house, who the hell are you?"

I pretend I'm in a three-piece suit instead of clothes from a lingerie store and hold out my hand. "Logan Carpino. We spoke on the phone."

He tips his head, and his eyes narrow. He also does

not take my proffered hand and crosses his arms. "Gotta say, you are not at all what I was expecting. I also didn't expect you to be here, especially during a blizzard. You told me you'd be here after Christmas."

I mirror his stance and pretend I'm wearing underwear. "When the weather shifted, I changed my flight mid-trip. My luggage didn't make it. I'm making do."

"I can see that," he deadpans, but he won't stop glaring at the mattress situated in front of the fireplace.

It goes without saying, I've made better first impressions.

Moving on. "I'm sure you've had a busy few days. Demi said you were working."

"Dad?"

We both turn to the opening of the family room. Water is dripping from Demi's hair, she's wrapped in a towel, and for the first time in my life, my desire to make a prank call to nine-one-one shoots through the roof just to get her dad out of the house. But it doesn't have anything to do with wanting to rip that towel off to have my way with her.

It does have everything to do with the look on her face. She's not embarrassed for me to be here while her dad is too. She's guarded, and my gut tells me it has everything to do with me just asking her to travel around the world with me.

Sure, we've only known each other for a few weeks. And most of that was long distance. But from everything I've learned about her since I crashed into her tree, I'm sure this is all about me pushing too hard, too fast.

I should ease up. I should give her space. Fuck knows, I haven't ever wanted anyone enough to make a move on them unless it was one hundred percent convenient, and even then I rarely gave a shit.

Avery said to go with my gut. I'm going for it.

"You didn't tell us you had company for Christmas." It's not a question. It's an accusation.

Demi takes a step forward. "Dad, this is Logan Carpino. He came a few days early—we were snowed in like everyone else."

The sheriff turns his glare from the mattress to me. "I'm sure you were."

"Sheriff—" I start.

"You can call him Joel," Demi interrupts.

I look to her dad, and he rolls his eyes.

"Joel," I start again. "I know what this looks like. I also know your daughter had a bad experience recently. You and I talked about that." I look at Demi. She bites her lip and white knuckles her towel. I continue speaking to her dad but don't look away from her tentative blue eyes. "Demi is as smart as she is gorgeous. She challenges me in ways no one has. I like that. This has been the best Christmas, and I don't want it to end." She widens her eyes and gives her head a slight shake. I think she's silently begging me to shut the fuck up, but I refuse. I look back to her dad. "I have another month on my project in Sydney. Demi can work from anywhere, and I've asked her to come with me."

"Logan," Demi hisses.

Joel shoots her a glare. "You said no, right?"

She narrows her eyes on her dad.

The sheriff raises his voice. "You're not going to Australia with a man you hardly know."

"Dad, you can't tell me what to do. And I know

Logan. Just for your information—both of you—I haven't decided."

"It's only for a month," I try.

"It's a whole damn month," her dad growls.

Her eyes fall and she pulls in a big breath. "Dad, why did you stop by?"

Joel throws his arms out wide. "To check on you, Demetria. I thought you were stuck by yourself in a blizzard for days. I see I was wrong."

I hold my hand up. "Whoa. Don't take this out on Demi. She didn't know I would be here early. I surprised her."

His expression hardens. "Like my girl would tell you to leave in the middle of a damn snowstorm. I don't need another jackass pushing his way into her life."

"Dad, stop," Demi warns. "Go. I'm sure you have citizens to check on who need you. I'm fine. We're fine. I'll call you and Mom later."

Joel glares at me before stalking across the room to his daughter. "Are you sure you're okay?"

Demi reaches up and kisses his cheek. "I know what happened with Sam freaked you out. But I'm fine. I wouldn't let Logan be here if I didn't want him here."

"Don't tell me you're thinking about going with him," Joel growls.

"I haven't decided. But when I do, it will be what I want, without input from anyone else."

I let out a silent breath. She hasn't said no.

Yet.

"Get dressed. You'll freeze." Joel reaches down and places a kiss on his daughter's forehead before turning for the door and pins me with one last stare for the road. "Watch it."

"Bye, Dad," Demi yells, not at all concerned with the sheriff's threats.

"Nice to meet you too," I mutter and shut the door. I turn to Demi. "I'm going to cut your power so we can go back to the way things were yesterday."

She leans into the door jamb. "Things were easier when it was just the fire, bad food, and us."

"I can make that happen."

She shakes her head.

I move and don't stop until she's in my arms. "I don't give a shit what he says or thinks of me. I'm not backing down. I want you to come with me. Promise me you'll think about it. I have to leave tomorrow. We can get your travel Visa online in just a few hours."

She gives me her weight, and I gladly take it. At this point, I'm desperate enough, I'll gladly take anything she gives me as long as she doesn't cut me out. "I don't know, Logan. It's so fast. You'll be back in a month. It's not that long. We can pick up then. One holiday without power is nothing. What if you get tired of me? I'm actually very boring. I work, and work, and work some more. That's it."

"Interesting, since that's all I do too. The only difference is you do it from home, and I do it from everywhere but home. Let's spend the next month in Oz and see if we hate each other."

She rolls her eyes. "That's the most romantic thing anyone has ever said to me."

I drop my hand to her towel-covered ass and squeeze. "If you choose wisely, you can be romanced like this for a long, long time."

All I see is wet hair when her forehead lands on my chest.

Maybe I'm wearing her down.

"At least we weren't in the shower together when your dad got here. It was bad enough wearing your clothes."

She looks up and gives me a small smile. "Electricity means real life, and real life means you'll probably wear underwear, doesn't it?"

"I'll gladly stay commando in your presence for as long as you'll have me, baby." I shake my head. "Say you'll come with me, and I'll throw all my underwear into the Tasman Sea."

Her smile fades, but her fingers grip my shirt tighter.

"Demi," I push.

She reaches up to kiss me, but I take over. Her back is to the wall and her towel hits the floor before I let her mouth go. It's more difficult than anything I've done, but I don't touch her the way I want to ... the way I'm desperate to.

Instead, I tip my forehead to hers. "Don't say no. Whatever you do, just don't say no."

I let her go and move to the bathroom.

This is a form of misery I'm not used to.

EIGHTEEN
OPEN ENDED

Demi

The power is on, and my old furnace is hacking away like it's smoked three packs a day for the last five decades.

It might not be far from the truth.

I found a frozen lasagna in the freezer and I was able to cook Logan a meal that wasn't warmed over the campfire.

My mom and dad have been relentless, leaving me a million voicemails. Both of them are checking on me since I have a male overnight guest they didn't know about. What every message had in common was they knew I wasn't going to Australia. How they were sure I was too *pragmatic*, *responsible*, and, they didn't say it, but *boring*, to up and do something so wild, crazy, and irresponsible.

They're right on all counts. I'm all those things.

And all those reasons are holding me back.

I hate myself for it.

Logan must have sensed the internal war I'm fighting. He's proved once again that he's pretty damn perfect, because he hasn't asked me again to come with him. Instead, he brought us back to the magical place we found when it was just us in the middle of a snowstorm.

We didn't move the mattress back to my bedroom. We didn't turn the lights on. No TV. Neither of us checked emails or tried to get caught up on work.

The only thing running other than my old furnace are the fairy lights twinkling on my skinny, bare Christmas tree.

The sun set hours ago.

I fell asleep in Logan's arms, wearing nothing but a tank and panties. Everything might be the same, but my old house is nice and warm tonight.

The New Year has come and gone, and Winter Falls is back to business as usual. It's my last night with Logan. You'd think I'd toss and turn, but I don't. I'm sure that will happen tomorrow when I'm by myself again … when he's gone and I'm regretting my boring and pragmatic and responsible personality traits that I just can't shake.

My eyes flutter open when a warm hand drags my panties down my hips. Lips and a tongue assault the skin below my ear, and a tremor of the best sort ripples down my back when I feel his cock on the bare skin of my ass.

His deep baritone flutters across my skin. "Don't move."

I nod and my breath goes shallow.

"You're wet for me," he notes. My panties are tangled around one ankle as he plays with me, spinning me into a flurry of emotions that are as deep as the snow outside. "Gonna miss this, baby. Gonna miss you more than anything."

"Logan—" I try to turn to look at him but he stops me when his long, hard cock slides into me from behind, stretching me and filling me in a way I never want it to end.

His hand slides over my hip and between my legs. When his fingers find my needy clit, I arch, wanting more of him—as much as I can get.

He slides in and out of me, excruciatingly slow when all I want is more.

Faster.

Harder.

One more souvenir … before he leaves.

Before it's over.

He continues his torture until he can't take it any longer.

His fingers circle faster. His cock slams into me harder.

"This doesn't have to end."

His words… They pierce and slay me.

"Don't let it end. Give me your trust, hacker. Time doesn't matter, you know me. All of me, in and out."

I lean my head on his chest, his lips hit my shoulder, and his teeth sink into my skin. I come instantly, and he follows shortly after. His body moves with reckless abandon, and he holds nothing back.

My moans cut through the quiet room, trailed by a growl that vibrates through me where we're connected.

I'm spent when he comes, limp and wrapped in his arms with his muscular body cradling me. He holds me tight to his chest and doesn't pull out. My breathing hasn't evened yet when I hear the crinkle of paper.

The source of that noise is forced into my fingers, and my eyes fly open. "What's this?"

He presses his lips to the back of my head. "Open ticket."

I do my best to read the paper in the darkened room. "Ticket?"

"I'm giving you every opportunity to not break me. No one's ever had the power to break me, baby, until you."

"Logan—"

"I'd rather you use it today. I'm not above guilting you. It's not like I've ever asked anyone to travel around the world to spend time with me, let alone for a whole month. I can barely stand my own family for a week."

I hold the piece of paper to my chest that holds all my hopes and fears. "I don't know what to say."

"Say you'll leave with me. I don't want to miss a minute with you."

I pause before whispering, "Honestly?"

He gives me a squeeze. "That depends."

"I'm scared."

"It's just a plane ride and a vacation. Don't make it into anything more." He pulls out, and I miss him instantly. I roll to my back, and he's warm everywhere when he covers me. "I'm going to shower. My Uber will be here in a couple of hours. Pack up your laptop and come with me."

He kisses me once more and doesn't give me a chance to say anything else.

In all his bare beauty, he stalks away from what has become our bed in front of the fire.

And I fist my open-ended ticket tighter than I have anything ever before.

NINETEEN
AIRPORT

Logan

My Uber honks.

Again.

I'm wearing the same thing I did when I got here, the first time in days I've actually worn my own clothes. If I could push back my return to Sydney, I would. Hell, there was a moment in the middle of the night when I woke up and watched her sleeping that I wondered if I would be committing career suicide if I just quit. It's not like I don't have head-hunters calling me all the time. The offers I've gotten from our clients have been even better. I have plenty of money, I could wait out my six-month non-compete and live in the mountains.

Then I wondered how the headlines would read if I just kidnapped her, whisked her off to Australia for a month, but didn't do the weird shit that kidnappers do.

Though, I'm open to other kinds of weird shit.

The scenarios that ran through my mind were whacked.

And not one of them included this. My hacker standing in front of me, not packed, not dressed, and definitely not going anywhere, let alone prepped for a twenty-four-hour trip around the world.

"It's just a month," she whispers.

I want to shake her.

"We'll text and we'll talk. You'll be back, and we'll pick up where we left off."

I stuff my hands in my pockets. If my hands were free, I know for a fact I'd pick her up and throw her over my shoulder. But I don't need that kind of attention from the sheriff.

Plus, I want her to want to be with me as much as I want to be with her. And that has not one thing to do with ego or pride. When it comes to her, I don't give a shit about that. But for this to be good for her, she needs to do it on her own.

I've decided I've never really wanted anything before now. The need for her that's coursing through my veins right now confirms it.

I want Demi, and I'll do whatever I have to do to make that happen.

Her voice is rough with emotion. "Please don't look at me like that."

The Uber honks. What the fuck, he's on the clock. I'd give my year-end bonus for a few extra moments with her.

"Look at you like what?" I ask. If this is it, I can't not touch her. I close the distance and push her to the wall beside the door. Just like it has since she met me in the snow when I crashed into her tree, my body hums, and my fucking insides ignite for her. I lean down and drag my tongue across her bottom lip. "Like there's nothing more I've ever wanted?"

"Stop."

"Why?" I demand. "If you want to be with someone who will make you feel okay about time apart, you hacked the wrong guy, baby."

Her eyes well and overflow, a tear dripping between us. "I'm not used to this."

My voice turns to stone. "Don't you trust me? I'm not that other guy, Demi."

Her grip on my shirt tightens. "I know that."

"Then don't treat me like it."

"I'm sorry."

The Uber honks, and as much as I'd pay him to sit there all damn day, I have a flight to catch, and unlike hers, my ticket is not open ended.

My jaw turns to stone, and I bite my lip. There are so many things I want to say. Hell, what I want to do is beg.

I press my lips to hers, and they move with mine—with as much desperation as I feel. Why the hell she's resisting, I have no idea.

I untangle her fingers from my shirt and can't look into her hazy blues. This is not the last memory I want of her for a whole month. I kiss her forehead once more, desperate for a last touch, which will not be nearly enough to get me through the next several weeks.

I say nothing and concentrate on not ripping her old door off the hinges when I leave.

"Logan," she calls after me.

I climb into the back of the Uber and slam the door.

The driver looks at me through the rearview mirror. "Airport?"

I nod. "International terminal."

He puts the car in drive, and we move over the snow packed streets.

I don't look back.

I don't dare. I don't trust myself.

TWENTY

CODE RED

Demi

I focus on my screen—the same one I've been staring at for way too long. My current project is due to the client next week, and I'm not even close to finishing.

Focus? I don't know the meaning.

Sleep? No way.

Food? I can't stomach a thing.

Not even the Christmas cookies my mom sent home with me when we were finally able to celebrate. But following the best Christmas ever, it was painful to be happy. My parents did everything they could to cheer me up. When they kept pressing and pressing, I told them I was just too conflicted for a belated Christmas, when secretly, I wished I was on a whole other continent.

Logan calls me constantly. He texts multiple times a day. He tells me how much he misses me, what we would be doing if I were there, and asks me the status on my last online date-turned-fiasco, Sam the creeper.

I assured him Sam has remained out-of-sight, out-of-mind.

What I don't tell Logan is how I miss him more than anything and that regret claws at me. It's digging its talons in deep, becoming more and more painful as the days click on.

It's a new year.

I love the start of a new year. I always have. There's something beautiful about a fresh start, a new lease on life. New goals, new challenges, and new opportunities.

But not this year. I've fallen into a depression because I think I've fucked up my fresh start and stomped on my chance at new opportunities, all because I'm a big, fat chicken.

I'm so stupid.

"What's wrong?"

Posey stops by, but I refuse to look at her—she can read me like a good romance novel and will know my level of misery is at code red. "I'm afraid I'm going to miss my deadline and I've never missed a deadline."

"You need a change of scenery. Get dressed. You can grab dinner with me and Eli, then come back with a fresh brain."

I shrug, staring at the coding in front of me that would be easier to crack if I could concentrate long enough to follow the paths. "I'm not hungry."

"Hey, what's this?"

I hear paper crinkle and spin in my office chair. The moment I see her reading my wrinkled open-ended promise, I panic. "Give that to me."

She turns to keep it out of my reach. "Is this a plane ticket voucher?"

"Posey—"

She turns to me. "To Australia?"

I step back and cross my arms.

She tosses the piece of paper to my desk. At this point, I'm surprised it's readable. I've crumpled it, thrown it away, dug it from the trash, slept with it, agonized over it, and might've shed a couple of tears on it.

Not that I'm being dramatic or anything.

"You made it sound like your Christmas romp with the Force of Nature was a one-off. But heartbreak is written all over your face, and I'm pretty sure you've been crying on that ticket."

Shit, I guess dry tears really do show on paper.

"What did that asshole do to you?" Posey demands.

I'm quick to shake my head. "Nothing. And he's the farthest thing from an asshole. He's sweet and perfect—in every way. His brother and brother-in-law created that profile as a joke. That and the fact that you swiped it when neither of us were interested in meeting anyone is surreal."

She motions to the ticket that continues to taunt me with promises of … a future? "And he wants you to go to Australia with him? He bought you a ticket?"

I take a deep breath. "Yes."

She spears me with a glare. "And you're still here? What the hell is wrong with you?"

"You know me." I shrug, because there's no other explanation needed.

Her eyes soften, and she moves across the room. I'm taken aback, because I find myself in the arms of my childhood friend who is not a hugger. "I love you, Demi."

I give her a squeeze. "Love you too."

But she jerks back, grips my shoulders, and her face turns hard. "But you're an idiot. There aren't enough men on this mountain for you to hang around here forever. You can do your sneaky, hacker shit from anywhere. You're one of the smartest people I know, but sometimes you can be blind. So now you're going to sit around here, miserable, waiting for Sambal the freak to try and make another move on you?"

"Hell, no." I pull away from her and cross my arms. "Just … yuck. How can you even say that?"

"Because that's what you're doing. For you, sticking your toe outside of your comfort zone is like eating chips over your keyboard." I cringe. Crumbs and technology do not play well. There's nothing more disgusting than a dirty keyboard. Her eyes widen, and her hands hit her hips. "See?"

"Okay, fine. It freaks me out. Are you happy?"

She hitches a foot.

"What?" I demand.

She narrows her eyes and studies me. Then, she nods slowly.

"Stop it," I say. "You're freaking me out."

Then, she moves.

I turn as she brushes past me in a rush. "Wait. Where are you going?"

She doesn't answer as she heads straight to my bedroom. When I get there, she's dragging my suitcase out from beneath my bed.

"What the hell?"

She talks as she moves. "We need to work fast. I have plans with Eli, but I'd be a shit friend if I allowed you to sit here on this mountain alone and wallow in your depression."

She digs through my drawers, dumping loads of panties, bras, and all my favorite clothes, made up of mostly athleisure, since I work from home.

"If you want anything in particular for the next month, I suggest you lend a hand. I've got three hours. That's enough time for me to dump you at the airport and be back to Eli." She stands and turns to me. "Get your passport. I have no clue where that is, but you're gonna need it."

"Posey—"

She jams random shit into my suitcase and turns to me. "Look, you'll thank me. On the small chance this doesn't work out, think of it as a short vacation to a country you'd never go to on your own. But if it does work out, I'll be toasting you at your wedding and again at your fiftieth anniversary. You can thank me then."

I open my mouth, but nothing comes out.

"Demi." Her tone is firm, yet loving. "I've known you your whole life. You're not a dumbass, you just need a push. This is me giving you one."

I think of Logan and the look on his face when I turned him down. I think about the days we spent together.

"Get your passport, girl."

I think about his phone calls ever since. And my new state of depression.

What the hell am I doing to myself? What am I doing to Logan?

I exhale and whisper, "Okay. I'm going to Australia."

A grin creeps over her beautiful face. "Hell, yeah,

you are. And we're leaving in ten. I've got a new man I need to get back to. That blizzard was the best thing to happen to us."

Holy shit.

I'm doing this.

I'm going to Australia … to Logan.

Maybe I'll surprise him. What the hell am I going to tell my parents?

I don't have time for that now. I need to get a travel Visa and find my passport. I'll worry about everything else on the way to the airport.

TWENTY-ONE

MINE

Logan

"Fuck." I close my laptop harder than necessary. "You were supposed to be prepared. Your team had the entire holiday to get their shit together."

Lina's eyes slide to the right, and she addresses the new Chief Executive Officer here in Sydney who will take over when we're done with the reorg. "Ian, can you excuse us for a few moments?"

Ian is more than happy to leave. He barely nods and grabs his shit, the door practically biting his heels when he slams it shut.

I get up and stalk to the windows.

Lina's tone is even and calm as always. "It's Wednesday, Logan."

"I know what day it is," I snap. I know all too well. All I've done since I got back was stare at the clock and calendar—that is, if I'm not staring at my phone. The fucking device I've never allowed to have a hold on me, but now that motherfucker is like a noose. I have every damn notification on and still check it every five minutes.

I haven't heard from Demi in approximately thirty-two hours and—

How long did that meeting last before I lost my shit? I turn to grab my phone off my desk.

Yep. Thirty-two hours and forty-three minutes.

And she still hasn't called or texted. I even opened the damn Force of Nature app in case she decided to switch back to that.

I've been ghosted by my hacker.

I don't even recognize myself.

"I thought you might need a reminder that before we left for Christmas, the team decided to come back and collaborate tomorrow. Which means you biting someone's head off today is too early. To be fair, that needs to wait one more day."

I close my eyes and pinch the bridge of my nose. "I hate last-minute shit."

"Yes, but not everyone dedicates their time off to work, like you."

I turn to glare at the woman who puts up with more of my shit than anyone should have to. "Are you rubbing it in that I don't have a life?"

I actually catch her off guard. She tips her head and softens her tone, reminding me of my mother, who I apparently made cry at Christmas. "No. I would never. I'm saying you choose work every waking minute. Not everyone does."

I didn't choose work over the holiday, and it was really fucking perfect. I stuff my hands in my pockets, because making my mom cry is bad enough. I've never seen Lina cry and I need to keep it that way.

"Sorry. I didn't mean it like that. We both know I have no life."

She stands and takes a couple of steps to my desk. "You've been off ever since you got back from the States. I think when we get back there, you need to take some time off."

If I'm obsessing over Demi now, I can't imagine what it would be like if I didn't have a job to focus on. That sounds like hell. What I can't tell Lina is that while I was at Demi's, I secretly put out some feelers and am already getting offers. But even so, in the last thirty-two hours, I haven't answered any of them. "I'll be fine."

Lina looks at me as if she knows something she shouldn't. Finally, she shakes her head. "Go home. Go for a run, hit the gym, do whatever you do to unwind. I've seen it, Logan. You'll burn out too young. I think it's time for some serious self-reflection."

I look up and smirk. "Thanks, Mom. I'll see you tomorrow."

She picks up her stuff and turns for the door. "And don't worry, I'll apologize to Ian for you. I'm a pro at making you look good."

I look down and check my damn phone again. Two minutes have passed and not a single notification. Where are they when you want them? "I know you are. It's one of your many superpowers."

"I don't know what you'd do without me," she sing-songs as she walks out of my office. She's not wrong.

Lina probably knows me better than anyone. I should leave and hit the gym, go for a run, or do something I haven't taken the time to do since I've been here—escape to the beach. I should do anything other than obsess over Demi. Right now, I'm jealous of her hacking skills, because I'd really like to know what she's doing right now.

I should call her dad. Have him check on her.

Shit.

I can't believe it hasn't crossed my mind until now. What if that guy came back? What if he got to her?

The thought grips me, and I pick up my phone to pull up her dad's number. He wasn't happy to see me at her house, but I don't give a shit. I need to know she's okay.

He answers immediately and knows who's calling. "Are you still wearing my daughter's clothes, Carpino?"

I'll never live that down and choose to ignore his comment. "Sheriff, I was wondering if you've heard from Demi. She hasn't answered my calls or texts. I'm concerned, especially given the fact that guy has a sick fixation on her."

I hear a car door slam in the background. "You haven't heard from Demi?"

I stand and move back to the windows. The last of the day's glow is reflecting off the Harbour and lights are dotting the buildings all around. "No. Did something else happen with VanDervleté?"

"My girl isn't going to have to worry about that cocksucker anymore. He's been slapped with a restraining order and assured me he's moving on. Turns out, he wasn't an engineer after all—lied on that godforsaken app. He was bussing tables at a dive in the next town over and preys on tourists. I've tied him to three separate complaints in neighboring counties. As soon as he got wind of that, he skipped town. In fact, he was out of here before the blizzard hit. My Demi doesn't have to worry about him anymore."

I drag a hand through my hair. "That's good news. I can't tell you how relieved I am."

"I'm glad you are, but I'm not. My only daughter seems to enjoy meeting strange men on dating apps, and I've gotta tell you, I'm not too pleased with your profile."

My eyes pop open. "No, that was a mistake."

"A mistake," he echoes.

"Yeah. See, my brother and brother-in-law like to be assholes. They created that profile as a joke."

"Settle down there, Capital P. Demi told me. And, I talked to your mom."

I freeze. "You talked to my mom? What the hell?"

"Why do you think? Demi is coming down from Sambal the asshole and then attracts you, who ends up being an overnight guest who likes to wear her clothes."

"Whoa," I warn. "I did not enjoy wearing her clothes. I lost my suitcase and there was no electricity. For God's sake, we were stuck in a blizzard. It's not like I could make a trip to the mall."

"Your mom assured me wearing women's clothing is not common for you."

"No, it's not." I'm fucking sick of this. "Can we get back to Demi? Where is she?"

"Son, if you don't know where my daughter is, that's your own problem."

"Logan."

As if on cue, her voice comes out of nowhere, and I spin on my heel.

Her hair is a mess on top of her head, her clothes are wrinkled, and she looks exhausted. But she's here.

She's here.

My online-dating-nightmare-turned everything is standing in my office with the biggest suitcase I've ever seen.

Here, in Sydney.

"What are you doing here?" As soon as the words pop out of my mouth, I want to punch myself in the junk.

"Dammit, Carpino. She said you bought her a ticket!" her dad bellows in my ear.

A small smile settles on her beautiful lips. Her lips that I missed like they were my own severed limb. "You did buy me an open-ended ticket."

I shake my head. "I meant to say, *you're here.*"

She nods as Sheriff Benjamin keeps berating me. "You'd better not turn out to be an asshole. Your mama and Demi assured me you're not, but that doesn't mean I like my daughter being halfway around the world with a stranger."

I don't take my eyes off her, and there's nothing I want more than to end this fucking phone call so I can welcome his daughter properly to the southern hemisphere. "I'll take care of her. I'd lay my life down for her."

Demi's smile grows, and her dad drawls, "That's what she said."

"I'll talk to you soon, Sheriff. Thanks for the update on VanDervleté."

I don't wait for him to say goodbye and disconnect. I'll have to fix that later, but I can't wait another second to touch her.

Tossing my cell to the sofa, reality sinks in when my hands touch her face and pull her lips to mine. I plunge my tongue in her mouth. She tastes like mint and coffee and french fries, a cocktail that my dick enjoys, because it instantly comes to life after the last depressing few days I've endured. She drops her bag and purse to the floor, and I kick my office door shut behind her.

I pull my lips away and look down at her. "You haven't answered, and I've been going fucking crazy. But you're here. I can't believe you're here. "

"I stink and need to brush my teeth. That flight is no joke. But thanks for the first-class seat."

I reach around her and flip the lock. "I wouldn't care if you crawled through the desert for a week."

I rip the button and zipper on her jeans and start to push them down. "Logan, we can't do this here."

"We can. The door's locked and no one wants in here anyway. Everyone but my assistant hates me, especially since I got back."

She smiles and kicks off her shoes. "They just don't know you."

I hike a brow as I wrestle with her jeans. How the hell do women have any type of circulation wearing shit like this? "Yeah? And you know me?"

I untangle one foot and give up on the other. I pick her up and she wraps her legs around my waist. When we're eye to eye, she dips her fingers in my hair and holds tight. "I'm here, aren't I?"

I grip her bare ass with both hands and squeeze. "Finally. I should put you face down over my desk and spank you for not calling and driving me mad."

Her blue eyes flare. We did a lot of shit while stranded in the blizzard, but I never pushed it to anything like that. I'm about to take it back when the end of her lips tip. "Don't make empty threats, Logan."

I narrow my eyes and contemplate moving to my desk. I might if my dick weren't begging for her. I reach under her ass and free myself. "I had no idea you'd be into that. We'll explore that thought later, though. Not sure I can wait another minute for you."

My cock springs free, and her wet pussy teases its tip. A minute ago, I was wondering if she ditched me for good, and now there's nothing in my way from making her mine.

I sink two fingers inside her, and Demi's head falls to the wall with a *thunk*. "I missed you. I'm sorry I wasn't here sooner. I'm sorry I didn't leave with you when you asked."

I pump her with my fingers, give her clit a circle, and taste the skin below her ear. "You're here. That's all that matters."

"Please, Logan. I want you." She pulls her knees up as she tries to get more leverage on my hand and lifts her head. Her eyes are at half-mast and mirror the need coursing through me. "Don't make me wait."

"You first." I focus on her clit, and she arches her back. "There you go. How much did you miss me, hacker?"

"From the moment you walked out my door." Her breaths come quicker and more shallow. "I couldn't sleep, work, or eat. No one has ever affected me like this. You left, and I was lost."

"Fuck, baby. You're soaked." I circle her swollen clit faster and she moves as best she can from where I have her pinned to the wall. Her breath catches, and her pussy starts to spasm. "There you go."

My cock replaces my hand. I groan.

Wet.

Tight.

Mine.

I pull out and push back in, feeling her pussy milk me, grip me, and take every inch as if I'm hers. She continues to come, and I don't hold back. Not having her for days has made me desperate in a way I've never felt.

Her nails bite into the skin at my nape, and her jaw goes slack. Neither of us can form words. My grip under her thighs tightens as I take her—over and over and over. My balls feel like they're going to explode right before I come.

I surge into her one last time and give her all my weight, pressing her to the wall to steady us both. Resting the side of my face to hers, our breaths mingle as she holds on with unsteady limbs.

After a few moments, her whisper brushes my lips. "Thank you for the Aussie welcome."

I look into her eyes. "Thanks for not ghosting me."

"I don't think that's possible. Not now." Her fingers grip my hair, and I take her mouth for a deep kiss.

"Let's get out of here. The jetlag is going to set in soon. How did you find my office?"

She hikes a brow. "How do you think? I hacked your phone."

I shake my head, and she proves I chose wisely when I decided she was the one. "You might be drop-dead gorgeous, Demetria Benjamin, but it's your brain that made me go crazy for you."

TWENTY-TWO
HAPPY SCALE

Demi
Three weeks later
Wategos Beach, Australia

Comfort zones are a scary thing.

I've thought more and more about my comfort zone in the past month. I've been fine in my zone for years. I can't complain. I have my family, a couple of friends, a business I've worked hard building, and hobbies right out my back door that have always brought me joy.

Have I been happy?

I guess.

I mean, yes. On the scale of happy, I was on it.

But a month ago, I didn't know there was a scale.

All I can say as I lounge on a beach in the southern hemisphere with my personal Force of Nature, is there's definitely a scale, and I'm currently sitting pretty at the top of it.

"You can suck my cock at any time. Just say the

word, hacker. No need to stare."

I push up from where I'm lounging on my stomach and rest my head in my hand. "I was just thinking how sweet you turned out to be and not an asshole at all, then you go and make a comment like that."

"I'm just being honest." He flips his sunglasses off, closes his laptop, and adjusts his now thick cock in his swim trunks. "And hopeful. You can't hate a guy for trying."

"Maybe later." I lick my lips and drag my gaze up his body that's now a darker color of olive than it was when I got here. Apparently Logan Carpino didn't understand the notion of down time from work. I get it. I usually work fifty-to-sixty hours a week myself.

But since I got here, I've cut back and made Logan do the same. It's crazy how the same shit gets done when you have other things to focus on.

Like each other.

He reaches over and palms the bare globe of my ass and squeezes. "I'm going to miss this when we get back to the mountains."

"I don't plan to forget my ass in Australia. It's coming with me."

He shakes his head, his dark eyes following the movement of his finger as it dips below the thin fabric of my thong. Like every time he touches me, my insides come alive and my heart flutters … for him.

When he drags his middle finger between my cheeks and circles the very sensitive area he very much enjoys playing with, he keeps talking. "No, but the last time I checked, we'll be returning to snow that's still knee-deep. I'm not going to see you laying around in this for a while."

I clench around his finger, and he smiles, pulling it

lower between my legs. "What are you doing?"

He gives his head a small shake. "No one's around. I paid a pretty penny to make sure of it."

My eyes widen. "So you could do this?"

"So I could do a lot of things. This," he makes easy work of pulling the minuscule piece of material to the side, "is just one of them. Open up, baby."

I bite my lip and rest my cheek back down on my towel. He's right, there's no one around. We've got the house and private beach that spans a mile for the next three days. Logan does not mess around when it comes to accommodations.

So I do as he says. I open, and he takes full advantage.

He swings his legs over his lounger and his feet land in the sand between us. I might as well be naked. His big hand is cupping everything. His fingers move between my sex and clit and my ass. Slow, methodical, and not at all in a hurry even though we're outside. He brushes my hair from my face as his other hand works between my legs.

"I want to ask you something," he starts.

My eyes fly open, and I fight for a breath. "Now?"

His touch goes from soft to firm as he cups me to lift my hips for better access. "Yes, now."

I start to close my eyes, but his touch startles me. With his other hand, he traces my lips with his thumb, cupping my chin softly. "I want to talk about the future."

Another swipe of my clit. My bikini thong is stretched to the max and I wonder if it will be trashed when he's done. It's one of my favorites, but I just don't care at the moment.

"The future," I mutter against his thumb, and

when I do, he presses in. When I look up, there's nothing but lust and pure Italian-American sexual desire rolling off him in waves. I bite down on his thumb.

His lips tip, but he only pushes his thumb in farther at the same time he pumps me with two thick fingers.

Holy hotness. He's everywhere.

"Suck," he demands.

I close my eyes and remember last night when I walked into the McMansion on the beach at sunset. I was wound tight with nervous energy not knowing where we were going, since Logan insisted on keeping it a surprise. I dropped to my knees and took him in my mouth. He was as surprised as I was.

I suck and lift my hips for more.

"Good girl." He works my clit as I suck his thumb. It's hard to forget where we are as the waves lap the shore, the breeze blowing through the palms, and the warm sun kissing my bare skin. "I'm taking a week off after we leave Australia, but then I have to be back in New York."

My eyes fly open, and I stop sucking. He circles my clit again and presses on my tongue.

"You should see yourself—so fucking hot. I might explode just watching you. Don't stop, baby." His warning hits me like a feather—soft and sweet and makes me want to bend over backward to do anything this man asks me to do. So, of course, I suck. "I want you to come to New York with me."

That stops me again.

He circles my clit faster, and my heart beats heavier than it ever has. "We'll take it one week at a time, but I have to be back and I don't want to be away from you."

At that, I suck harder.

"Is that a yes?"

My teeth sink into his flesh, but it's my clit that's rewarded. The thought of being away from him is painful, and it has nothing to do with the position I'm in right now, but everything to do with Logan making me the queen of the happy scale.

"Never been happier, baby," he croons as my breath leaves my body, I topple, falling over the edge he's kept me on. My jaw goes slack around his thumb and I gasp for air, moaning into the warm, Aussie breeze. Logan is relentless, doesn't let up, and works my orgasm until I'm spent.

I'm about to collapse into a lump of post-orgasmic mush when I'm up and flipped around. Face to face, I straddle his waist as he pulls my poor, abused bikini bottoms out of the way. He's already freed himself, so when he settles back into his lounger, I sink onto his cock.

I grip his biceps. "Logan—"

"Move," he demands, yet he all but takes care of it. His hands grip my hips, moving me up and down his cock, creating a new friction that builds low in my belly. He looks up at me, his beautiful dark eyes, two-day beard, and hair messy from the ocean. I thought shacking up in an apartment in Sydney with Logan Carpino was heaven, but this … this is like living a dream I didn't know I needed.

Craved.

This is life-changing.

What breasts I do have bounce in my tiny bikini top as he moves me vigorously, but I just don't care. I'm close. Again.

Every time with Logan is something new, something special, and something I don't want to end.

I grab his forearms for support, and my head falls back. A second orgasm flows through me, and this one might do me in. Logan pulls me to his chest, pressing me down on his cock, and I feel him come, pulsing inside me.

He falls back to his reclined lounger and brings me with him. Between the sex, the summer heat, and Logan, I'm beyond warm and love it.

My face is tucked to his neck, and our chests rise and fall as one. Logan's hands move rhythmically from my salty hair to my mostly bare ass in a way I wonder if he played a string instrument in high school.

I relax and decide to ask him about that later.

"Hacker?"

I smile into his neck. "Hmm?"

"Have you ever been to Nebraska?"

Besides my eyes flying open, I freeze. "No."

"Well, you're going next month. Winter Falls, Manhattan, Omaha. If I don't visit soon, my mom will come to New York, and trust me, that's something we want to avoid. And I'm so fucking sick of my family bugging the shit out of me about you, it's time."

I put my hands to his pecs and push up to look him in the eyes. "You want me to meet your family?"

I'm still impaled on his cock, so he holds my hips tight to keep me here. "Yes. The sooner the better. I mean, I have met the sheriff. It's only fair."

I put my hand to his cheek and lean in for a kiss. "What's happening, Logan?"

His fingers thread my hair and he deepens the kiss. He finally lets me up for air. "I'm doing what feels right. Does any of this not feel right to you?"

I pull my lip between my teeth and give my head a shake. I wouldn't change a thing if I could.

"Then go with it. And when you meet my family, remember you were into me before they barged their way into our shit. Promise me you won't hold them against me."

My eyes widen. "That bad?"

"Not bad. Annoying and in your face, but not bad. You'll get used to it." He lifts me from his cock, and I miss him instantly. "Come on. I'll clean you up in the ocean."

I do my best not to stumble and try to right my bottoms. "I think you ruined my bikini."

"I'll buy you a new one." He tucks himself back in his swim trunks and grabs my hand. Then he motions to our beautiful surroundings he arranged for the best long weekend ever. "Do you even need a bikini here?"

I make my way to the water and look back to our joined hands. With my free one, I reach behind me and yank the tie on my top. His eyes widen as it falls and I toss it to the sand.

"You'd better be careful, hacker. I might just keep you forever."

I look back to the water, a color of turquoise I've never experienced in real life. So clear and so beautiful, nothing could capture this moment better than my memory. I'll never forget these days with Logan. "Don't make threats you're not prepared to follow through on, Carpino."

With that, I'm swept off my feet the moment they touch water. My scream is swallowed by the ocean, but Logan's arms never leave me. When we come up for air, his mouth hits mine. When he lets go, we're both out of breath. "Baby, you're mine. You can call it magic, the Christmas spirit, or serendipity. I don't give a shit anymore. This is happening, it's happening fast, and I've never been more fucking thrilled with anything in my whole life."

With the warm ocean water surrounding us, I feel lighter and more alive than I ever have. And I know without a doubt, I'll do anything and go anywhere for this man.

I smooth his overly long dark hair out of his face. "I'm afraid to say things to you. I'm afraid it's too soon. And I'm afraid because I've never said them to anyone before."

His arms convulse around me. "Demi."

"How can I love someone I've only known for such a short time?"

Waves rock around us but Logan holds me steady, my bare chest pressed to his. "I don't know."

I start to pull away, but he won't let me out of his hold.

"Because I feel the same," he finishes. "I have no fucking idea how you did it, but you rocked my world and I'm not willing for it to go back to the way it was."

I hop off the ocean floor and wrap my legs around his narrow waist. "I love you."

His gaze moves from my lips to my eyes, as if he can't believe I just said what I did.

I mean, I can't believe it either. But if any moment seems like the right time, it's now.

"Never thought my life would start by being hacked. Love you, baby. So much."

And just like that, my life takes a turn.

From happy to deliriously blissful.

And all because of a force of nature.

TWENTY-THREE
A CARPINO CHRISTMAS

Demi
February 15th

"Wait! So you're telling us that Logan—my cousin, Logan Carpino, who's addicted to work and never does anything without analyzing it to death, then plans it out two years in advance—whisked you off in a helicopter for a spur-of-the-moment trip to one of Australia's most exclusive areas when you were in Sydney?"

I put my beer to my lips and take a gulp. It's not often I drink too much, but tonight might be the night. The Carpinos are … well, they're a lot.

I look back to Gabby, Logan's cousin, and shrug with a small smile. "I didn't know it was so out of character for him."

"*Out of character* is an understatement," Paige pipes in and takes a sip of her pomegranate margarita. "But I have a feeling you're exactly what our stick-in-the-mud cousin needs. All I know is Aunt Tia is beside herself. You should have seen her getting ready over the last week. I really thought Uncle Nic was going to come unglued."

I think I'm in a Christmas movie from hell. Trans-Siberian Orchestra blares over the sound system, and the biggest Christmas tree I've ever seen in someone's house stands tall next to the fireplace that extends to the second-story ceiling. The only reason I know it's a tree is because of its shape. It's covered from top to bottom in lights and ornaments and ribbon and family pictures from decades past. I don't blame Logan's dad for coming unglued. I'm sure they just put all this stuff away a month ago.

But when we arrived in Omaha this afternoon for the life-changing event of meeting the Carpinos, you'd never know yesterday was Valentine's Day. Logan's massive childhood home is decorated from top to bottom in white and gold. There's nothing traditional about Tia's holiday décor—not one stitch of red or green is in sight.

I hope she doesn't want to visit us in Winter Falls until I can start on my fixer upper.

Logan's dad is an architect and builder, and if the Carpino home is anything to go by, he's really good at what he does. I'm blown away and, quite frankly, a bit intimidated.

"Hey, it's okay." I look over when a gentle hand lands on my forearm. A tall, beautiful blonde leans in close. I can't remember her name, but she walked in with her own tall, dark Italian-American and three miniature humans who look just like her husband—twin boys with their younger brother. "Look, I've been around the Carpinos for most of my life, but when I was officially brought in *as* a Carpino, it was over-whelming to say the least. I got you, girl."

I look into her brilliant green eyes and admit, "I can't even remember your name."

She bites back a laugh. "Leigh. I'm married to Tony. Don't worry, ask me as many times as you need. No one should be required to remember this bunch on the first try."

That's no joke. There are so many kids creating their own force of nature, I can't even count them, let alone remember their names, or to whom they belong.

I drink the last swig of my beer.

"I think you need another one." Paige gets up and leaves the huddle I've been forced into without even asking if I wanted another drink. Bless her. I'm going to need it.

"All I'm going to say is, I have no idea who that man is over there who is impersonating my big broth-er." I turn to Avery. I do remember her name. She's Logan's younger sister, and I internet-stalked her before I ever hacked Logan. Her gaze moves from the man who shook up my life for the better and settles the same eyes she shares with her brother on me. "He looks like Logan and sounds like Logan, but he is not the same Logan. I think you've reformed my big brother. And I've never seen my mom so happy. Not that she thought he needed reforming. You see," she shifts closer and lowers her voice, "Logan is mom's favorite. He can do no wrong in her eyes." Avery rolls hers. "Which, when you get down to it, he never does anything wrong. No one is closer to perfect than Logan. But with me around, everyone looks perfect."

"Don't listen to her. Avery is a songwriter and has only won a couple of GRAMMYs." Gabby gives her cousin a gentle push on the shoulder, looks back at me, and rolls her eyes. "She's such a failure."

"I meant before that. I dropped out of college, got knocked up, and married before I was twenty-one." Avery widens her eyes and bleeds sarcasm. "It's amazing my parents lived through it."

I'm not about to admit I already know everything there is to know about Avery Forester. She only wrote one of my favorite songs. And she's not kidding. When Logan took our suitcases to his childhood bedroom, every honor, metal, and accolade from his youth still decorates the space. Even his high school diploma, stating that he was valedictorian of his class, is front and center.

Paige returns and hands me another beer. I imme-diately take a drink, but don't have time to thank her, because the cross-examination continues. "Enough about Logan. Have you hacked into any companies that we know of? Like big ones? Please tell me you have."

I lick my lips and rub my nose, always a tell-tale of becoming tipsy. "I sign nondisclosures. Sorry."

"Logan told Mom and Dad all about what you do and how hard it is," Avery says. "Between you and the Quiz Bowl king slash president of the calculus club, you guys are gonna create little Einsteins. Mom will be ecstatic."

I bite my lip and thumb the platinum diamond ring Logan slid on my left ring finger last night after he made love to me. I'll never forget his words. "I'm no dumbass, hacker. Kismet, fate, serendipity … call it what you will. But I'm not fucking around when it comes to destiny. We're making this shit official."

He never even asked me to marry him. There was

no point. What's meant to be is meant to be. I'm officially moving to Manhattan next week, not that I've been apart from Logan since the day I barged into his office in Sydney. Winter Falls will be our vacation home, and it looks like with the changes coming about in Logan's career, we'll be able to go often.

I look back to the Carpino women. I'll remember their names eventually, but for now, they've welcomed me with open arms, and I'm thrilled. And just like every time I twist the two-and-a-half carat solitaire on my finger, I can't help the grin that breaks my face in two. "I've got to admit, I'm ecstatic too."

Gabby raises her cocktail. "Welcome to the family, girlie."

Yes, yes, yes, yes echoes as the group follows suit.

"There's never a dull moment, but you'll never be loved more," Paige adds. "To Demi Carpino!"

Whoops and hollers surround me, and I take another drink. This will take some getting used to, but in the end, it might just be a bonus to being Mrs. Logan Carpino.

Logan

"DO YOU SEE THAT?" Grant hisses before glaring at me. "They're over there comparing proposals. When did you become such a romantic sap and decide to ask her to marry you on Valentine's Day?"

I'm not about to admit to anyone that I planned for weeks to put a ring on Demi's finger last night, but had no fucking clue it was Valentine's Day until I woke up and saw a commercial for chocolate. I had to scramble my ass to find a decent bouquet of flowers and called in four favors and paid triple just to have dinner delivered to the apartment. Who knew the fake, Hallmark holiday was such a big deal that I couldn't even order food in the city that never sleeps?

So yeah, I slid a ring on her finger on the only holiday made for lovers. If kismet keeps slapping me in the face, I'll take it. Demi was so happy, she cried in my arms and started making plans immediately.

Jude slaps me on the shoulder as he raises a beer in his other hand. "I've got one word for you man: *elope*."

"No way," Grant hisses. "Mom cried when you missed Christmas, and now we have to sit around the tree for the second time in seven weeks just because she wants the memory of you being here for it. If you elope, you'll do her in."

Grant's right. I look around the home I grew up in. My mother redecorates this place more than most people switch out rolls of toilet paper. It's been that way all my life, but it seems she's in one of her anti-color phases. Every surface is lit up—there's enough food to feed my entire family until the real Christmas rolls around again. And the music is enough to nauseate the strongest stomachs. I wouldn't be surprised if Santa barged in here with a bag full of shit that no one needs.

"We're getting married in Winter Falls. Demi is moving to Manhattan for me—the wedding will be whatever she wants. Her property is amazing but the house needs work. This will be a good excuse to get that done and I can foot the bill without her balking. I told her my only requirement is that it happens as soon as the snow melts."

Tony says, "You don't have much time if you're going to gut her house."

"I'll send my mom. She'll get that shit done faster than anyone." Cam grins. "Seriously, man. Happy for you. When you know, you know. Fiancée, new job, no more globetrotting. No reason to fuck around when it comes to starting your life."

"Didn't take me long to realize that," I agree without taking my eyes off the woman who reformed me and gave me a life. Only, what I realize now, I wasn't waiting on my life to start.

I was just waiting on her.

My force of nature I didn't know I needed and a Christmas that changed my life forever.

EPILOGUE

Christmas morning
Four years later
Logan

The first light of day is peeking over the mountain range. It's not the blizzard I experienced my first Christmas in Winter Falls, but we got a decent amount of powder last night.

Much to the dismay of my mother, Demi and I have spent every Christmas here since I crashed into her tree that dark, snowy night. My wife has tried to get me to take a year off from the mountains to celebrate in Omaha with my family, but it hasn't felt right.

Maybe someday.

Maybe next year.

Next year will look a lot different than this one. Next year we'll have different priorities. One, in particular.

The last four years have brought balance to my life.

Demi.

A new job.

Most recently, moving up in Manhattan. I thought I already lived *up*. But when a penthouse went on the market two blocks from my office at the same time my wife informed me I'm going to be a father for the first time, I jumped on it.

It cost a fucking mint, but has five times the space of what we had. It's also close to the best private schools in the city, which will come in handy in a few years.

For a mountain girl, Demi has adjusted to the city and loves it. Hell, I grew up in the suburbs. For a math nerd and computer geek, I think we've done okay.

But we come here as much as we can. And since we gutted the place before our wedding, it's an easy place to escape to. I even had a whole house generator installed in case the electricity goes out.

Even so, every Christmas Eve, I drag our mattress in front of the fire. Not sure how long that will last, but when we're here, we'll do it.

I look back into the family room. She's still sleeping where I left her to feed the fire. Unlike four years ago, the house is plenty warm, and she's a fireball, baking my first child. Her hand rests on her bare belly that I've loved watching grow more than anything.

She also sleeps like a champ while she's pregnant.

I've got a few minutes, so I slip back into the kitchen and open my laptop. Maneuvering through three security layers my wife set up, I click on my email since Lina, who I demanded come with me when I started my new job, is on vacation. But the screen goes Christmas red and white and starts to swirl in circles like candy canes on speed.

What the hell?

**Don't even think about it, Carpino.
There will be no email today. Shut your laptop.
It's Christmas!**

I shake my head. My wife … of course she would hack into my laptop and block my email on Christmas.

"I told you, Logan. No working on Christmas."

I turn when I hear her and don't even try to bite back my grin. I've been caught red-handed. She pulls her tank over her belly and yanks up my pajama pants since none of hers fit her anymore. I prefer her in my clothes as opposed to the other way around. I told her I don't care how much she wants to recreate our first Christmas together, my days wearing her clothes are over.

I shut my laptop, like I was told. "I was just going to check my email before you woke up. Will you ever stop hacking me?"

She lifts on her toes, and I meet her for a kiss. "Never."

I wrap my arm around her, and my hand lands on her ass. "Merry Christmas, hacker."

She leans into my chest and looks out the picture window to the quiet, white morning. "It's beautiful. So much powder."

"Don't even think about it. We'll take a walk later, but you are not getting on a board."

She looks up at me and smiles. "I know. I'm more than happy to be patient. I can't wait to teach her to ski."

I frown. "Slow down. She's not even fully cooked yet. My daughter will not be falling down a mountain anytime soon."

She gives me a squeeze. "You might run the world

when it comes to investment banking, but the mountain is mine. She's going to love being on the slopes."

I sigh and decide I've got at least a couple of years until I have to fight that battle, but the thought of my baby girl crashing on the slopes…

"Logan," she calls for me.

I look down to her. "Hmm?"

"You're going to be the best dad. You've never been hotter."

My lips tip on one side. "Yeah?"

She nods and grins. "Yeah. You going into *protective Dad mode*? It makes me want you to knock me up all over again."

My dick swells. "You know, I have kept one Christmas tradition."

"What's that?"

I press my dick into her. "I'm commando. I think it's time we celebrate before the Sheriff and your mom get here."

"Love you."

I take her hand and pull her back to the mattress on the floor. "Love you, too, Mrs. Carpino."

Want more Carpinos?

Read Jude and Gabby's story:
Overflow – The Carpino Series, Book 1
Read Tony and Leigh's story:
Beautiful Life – The Carpino Series, Book 2
Read Cam and Paige's story:
Athica Lane – The Carpino Series, Book 3
Read Link and Avery's story:
Until Avery – A Carpino Series Crossover Novella

ABOUT THE AUTHOR

Brynne Asher grew up in the Midwest and now lives in Northern Virginia with her husband, three children and her perfect dog. When she isn't creating pretend people and relationships in her head, she's running her kids around and doing laundry. She enjoys cooking, decorating, shopping at outlet malls and online, always seeking the best deal. A perfect day in "Brynne World" ends in front of an outdoor fire with family, friends, s'mores and a delicious cocktail.

facebook.com/brynneasherauthor

twitter.com/BrynneAsher

instagram.com/brynneasher

WHAT TO READ NEXT

The Carpino Series

Overflow – The Carpino Series, Book 1

Beautiful Life – The Carpino Series, Book 2

Athica Lane – The Carpino Series, Book 3

Until Avery – A Carpino Series Crossover Novella

Killers Series

Vines – A Killers Novel, Book 1

Paths – A Killers Novel, Book 2

Gifts – A Killers Novel, Book 3

Veils – A Killers Novel, Book 4

Scars – A Killers Novel, Book 5

Souls – A Killers Novel, Book 6

Until the Tequila – A Killers Crossover Novella

The Dillon Sisters

Deathly by Brynne Asher

Damaged by Layla Frost

The Montgomery Series

Bad Situation – The Montgomery Series, Book 1

Broken Halo – The Montgomery Series, Book 2

Standalones

Blackburn

Printed in Great Britain
by Amazon

27428143R00123